THE FAMOUS FIVE AND THE HIJACKERS

THE FAMOUS FIVE are Julian, Dick, George (Georgina by rights), Anne and Timmy the dog.

There's no end to the excitement facing the Five when their flight to Brazil is diverted by hijackers. But their captors' plans go badly wrong when their plane crashes deep in the South American jungle, near a tribe with a reputation for shrinking heads.

It seems the Five have finally met their match – until a remarkable discovery gives them new hope and determination to escape.

Also available from Knight Books:

The Famous Five and the Hijackers

A new adventure of the characters created by Enid Blyton, told by Claude Voilier, translated by Anthea Bell

Illustrated by Bob Harvey

KNIGHT BOOKS
Hodder and Stoughton

Copyright © Librairie Hachette 1973

First published in France as *Les Cinq et les Pirates du Ciel*

English language translation copyright © Hodder & Stoughton
Ltd. 1985
Illustrations copyright © Hodder & Stoughton Ltd. 1985

First published in Great Britain by Knight Books 1985

British Library C.I.P.

Voilier, Claude
  The Famous Five and the hijackers.
  I. Title   II. Les Cinq et les pirates du ciel. *English*
  843'.914[J]   PZ7

  ISBN 0-340-36809-8

Printed and bound in Great Britain for
Hodder and Stoughton Paperbacks, a
division of Hodder and Stoughton Ltd.,
Mill Road, Dunton Green, Sevenoaks,
Kent (Editorial Office: 47 Bedford
Square, London WC1B 3DP) by
Hunt Barnard Ltd., Aylesbury, Bucks.

CONTENTS

Chapter One

THE MOST EXCITING HOLIDAY EVER

'How marvellous! How simply absolutely super! Hooray for the holidays! Hooray for us! And three loud cheers for my father – hip, hip, *hooray*!'

George was dancing up and down on the beach with glee. Her name was actually Georgina, but she hated it and would rather have been a boy. She did look rather like a boy, too, with her short, curly dark hair. She was wearing shorts, and her legs were tanned brown by the sun.

'Woof! Woof!'

Timmy, George's beloved dog, could tell that his mistress was pleased about something, so he wanted to show her that he was pleased too. He joined in her dance in his very own way, jumping up and down and chasing round her, wagging his tail like mad.

At last George had to stop and flop down on the

beach, out of breath. Her cousins were watching her, laughing. Julian, Dick and Anne had arrived in Kirrin the day before. Their Aunt Fanny and Uncle Quentin – George's parents – had a lovely house there called Kirrin Cottage.

Julian, who was tall for thirteen, pushed back the fair hair that had fallen over his forehead.

'Well, I know you're fond of Uncle Quentin, George, but I've never heard you give three cheers for him before!' he said.

'No,' Anne agreed with her big brother. She was the youngest of the four cousins. 'Uncle Quentin can be so strict, and you grumble when he scolds you, George!'

Dick laughed. He was the same age as his cousin George, and he looked rather like her. 'George grumbles about Uncle Quentin being strict when he tells her off or won't let her do what she wants – but it's quite different when he says he'll send her on a holiday trip to South America! *And* he's sending us three too, so I say three cheers for Uncle Quentin as well! Hip, hip, hooray!'

Everybody joined in the hip-hip-hooraying, including Timmy, who barked at the top of his voice. Timmy, after all, was one of the Five! The four cousins and Timmy nearly always spent their holidays together, and they had had lots of adventures at Kirrin. But these were certainly going to be the most exciting holidays ever! The children had done so well in their exams at school that Uncle Quentin thought they deserved a special treat. He had booked them places on a South American holiday for young people! Of course there would be couriers to look after the party of children, but no other grown-ups were going on the holiday. And it was to take George and her cousins all the way to Brazil – they were so thrilled they could hardly believe it yet. *What* an adventure for the Five!

'Just think,' said George, gazing out to sea, 'we'll soon be the other side of the Atlantic Ocean!'

Anne shivered slightly. 'I'm a little bit scared of such a long plane journey,' she confessed. 'There's so *much* of the Atlantic in between us and Brazil!'

Julian smiled kindly at his little sister. 'Honestly, Anne, anyone would think you were a terrible coward, to hear you talk!' he said. 'But the fact is, you're as brave as anyone. You've proved that lots and lots of times.'

Anne blushed, feeling very pleased at Julian's compliment. She had a sweet, sensitive nature, and she *was* rather timid – compared with George, anyway, who wasn't afraid of anything. Anne didn't like unusual, unfamiliar things to happen, but just as her brother said, when she actually found herself in a tight place she showed just how brave she could be.

Dick was like George – *he* didn't mind the unexpected, and he'd face any sort of danger. Julian was the most responsible of the four children. Unlike his cousin, he thought before he acted and, though George sometimes said he was being stuffy, she knew he was often right!

'Woof!' said Timmy. He seemed to think nobody was taking enough notice of him. 'Woof! Woof!'

George immediately gave him the attention he was asking for. She and her dog were devoted to each other. 'It's all right, Timmy, we're not leaving you behind,' she reassured him. 'Did you think we would? My father knows I wouldn't want to go to Brazil without you – I'd rather stay here in Kirrin!'

Dick dug his cousin playfully in the ribs. 'And *we* wouldn't want to go to Brazil without *you* – so in other words, if Uncle Quentin hadn't made sure old Timmy could go on the holiday as well, *none* of us would have gone!'

'Which would have been a great pity,' said Julian.

'You bet it would!' said George. 'I simply love the idea of travelling to foreign countries. Maybe I'll be a famous explorer when I grow up! I'm sure we'll see all sorts of exciting things in South America. My father says we fly straight to Rio de Janeiro, and when we get there we'll have three weeks being taken round the country. What fun it's going to be!'

Her cousins agreed wholeheartedly. They were as excited as she was! They went back up the path from the beach to Kirrin Cottage – they were going to be very busy packing for their thrilling holiday, because their plane left London Airport in three days' time.

When the great day came, Uncle Quentin and Aunt Fanny drove them to the airport. They found the couriers who were in charge of the young people going on the holiday, and there was their plane standing on the runway! It had SOUTH AMERICAN AIRLINES written in huge letters along its side. George said goodbye to her mother and father. All of a sudden she felt a little sorry they weren't coming as well, but she wasn't going to show it! Tender-hearted Anne, however, shed a few tears as she kissed her aunt and uncle goodbye.

'Goodbye, Aunt Fanny! Goodbye, Uncle Quentin! Oh, I'll miss you!' she said.

Julian and Dick said goodbye too, and then the children boarded their plane. A very nice stewardess showed them where to sit. Everyone was smiling broadly, except for George – and *she* was looking glum because Timmy had to be parted from her during the flight. There was a special compartment of the plane where animals had to travel, right at the back.

'Are you *sure* my dog will be all right?' she asked

11

the stewardess.

'Don't you worry, young man,' said the stewardess. Like many other people, she thought George, who looked so like a boy, *was* a boy! 'Your dog will be very comfortable, and I'll make sure he gets a nice bowl of dog-food during the flight.'

That made George feel a bit better. She relaxed, and looked round. She was sitting beside a window, next to Dick, and Julian and Anne had the seats just behind them. The rest of the plane was filling up with other young people, all talking and laughing excitedly at the tops of their voices.

'My goodness, what a racket! You'd think we were in the zoo!' said Dick, smiling.

Soon the stewardess asked the passengers to fasten their safety belts. The big aeroplane began to move along the runway. Feeling very excited, the children watched the airport buildings seem to move away from them. Could those two tiny little figures standing on one of the roof-top viewing areas be Aunt Fanny and Uncle Quentin, waving goodbye?

At last the plane took off. They were airborne, and on their way!

They flew over part of England first. George could see towns, fields, rivers and woods down below, looking just like toys. Then they were over the sea. After some time they saw land down below again: it was part of Spain, and Portugal.

It was announced that they were stopping briefly in Lisbon, and the children could go and have refreshments in the airport cafeteria. As the young people in the group drank their Coca-Cola or milk shakes, they started getting to know each other. Most of them were students or school-children who were having the holiday as a reward for good exam results, like George and her cousins. Some of them had been given the trip to Brazil as a birthday present. The children thought most of their companions looked very nice.

'I bet we make lots of new friends,' said Dick happily. 'The more the merrier, that's what I say!'

George went and got permission to visit Timmy while the plane was on the runway at Lisbon. She was pleased to find he really did seem to be very comfortable, and she was running back to join her cousins when she bumped straight into one of the couriers in charge of the party of children. She had heard the other couriers call this young man Josh. When she collided with him, he snapped at her. 'Can't you look where you're going?' he said crossly.

George apologised – but the young man pushed his way rudely past her towards a tobacconist's kiosk.

'Well! *He* doesn't look like being very cheerful company!' said George to herself.

She told her cousins about the incident once she

was back with them again. They took it in different ways. Sensible Julian, always the peacemaker, said it wasn't anything to bother about. 'I expect Josh was feeling nervous,' he suggested. 'After all, we're quite a large group going on this holiday, and he and the other three couriers have a lot of responsibility to bear. It can't be easy for them.'

'Still, he didn't have to be so rude!' Anne protested.

As for Dick, he laughed. 'If you're going to start picking quarrels with the couriers I can see we're in for an interesting time!' he told his cousin. 'You've got a terrible temper, you know!'

George flared up at once. She didn't realise that Dick was teasing her about her temper on purpose to make her lose it! He knew how easily she flew off the handle.

'What do you mean, "temper"?' she said crossly. 'This Josh person is rude to me, and then you say *I'm* the one who –'

But Julian interrupted. 'Calm down, both of you!' he said. He knew that George and Dick could argue with each other for hours – though they were really the best of friends. And George did calm down. Anyway, they had to go back on board the plane now, because it was nearly time to take off again.

This time the plane flew straight out over the Atlantic Ocean. The children could see blue waves with white crests down below, but then the plane climbed higher, and soon it was up above a layer of clouds that looked like cotton wool. What a strange sight!

Anne was enchanted. 'Why, it's like being in heaven!' she cried.

You could listen to music if you put a coin into a slot beside your seat. Julian found a coin and then put his earphones on. Meanwhile, Dick opened a magazine. George preferred to look around her. She was a very observant little girl, and she liked studying people's faces and trying to guess what they were like or what they were thinking from their expressions and the way they acted. Not far away from her own seat, Josh and two of the other three couriers were all talking to each other.

'I don't like Josh's face a bit,' she thought. 'He looks rather like a bull getting ready to charge, with that square jaw and solid forehead of his. I'd say he was proud of his physical strength, but not really all that bright! I'm surprised they picked him to be in charge of a group of young people!'

The second courier was called Luke, and he seemed to be rather serious and thoughtful. He wasn't as athletic-looking as Josh, but he was rather elegantly dressed. The third courier, Marco, was short, thin and dark. He gesticulated as he talked, and had a slight foreign accent.

'I expect he's Portuguese, or partly Portuguese,'

George guessed. 'They speak Portuguese in Brazil, so I should think that's why *he* was chosen to go on this trip.'

Suddenly the stewardess asked for the passengers' attention, and told them a film would be shown. 'A Western,' she added.

A screen was let down at the front of the plane's cabin, and soon George was so caught up in the exciting story of the film that she forgot everything else.

After the film show the stewardesses brought round trays with meals on them. Then all the young people made themselves as comfortable as they could and tried to settle down for the night. The hours passed by – quickly if you were asleep, but slowly for those of the passengers who couldn't drop off.

George kept shifting about in her seat. She envied Dick, who was snoring happily away beside her! The thought of dear old Timmy was bothering her again. Poor thing – she was sure he must be terribly lonely and unhappy without her.

She looked at her fellow passengers in the dim light of the cabin. Daniel, the fourth courier, was sound asleep, but Josh, Luke and Marco had their eyes open.

'They look almost as if they were waiting for something,' George thought, stifling a yawn.

She closed her eyes – and this time, at last, she

did fall asleep, lulled by the sound of the plane engines. And all was quiet in the cabin.

Day was only just dawning when the stewardesses started going down the gangways, distributing breakfast trays. Julian leaned over the back of George and Dick's seats. 'Sleep well?' he asked them cheerfully.

'Like a log!' Dick told his brother in the same sort of tone.

'Wish I could say the same!' said George. 'I'm worried about Timmy – he *always* spends the night with me, and he must be wondering where I am!'

'Oh, don't worry! You'll soon be reunited with your dear little doggie!' Dick teased her. 'What a touching scene! We'll all weep buckets!'

'Idiot!' said George, throwing a punch at him, but she couldn't help laughing. 'Timmy is *not* a dear little doggie! It's just that I don't like being parted from him. Can't you understand that?'

'I can,' said Anne, leaning over to talk to George and Dick herself. But she was interrupted by a voice coming over the loudspeaker. It was the captain speaking from his cockpit.

'Good morning, ladies and gentlemen. In one hour's time we shall be landing in Rio de Janeiro. Will you please –'

But he never finished what he had been going to say. Nothing more came over the loudspeaker except for a confused sort of noise – it was hard to say just what it was. Julian wondered if the loud-speaker itself had gone wrong, or if the captain had suddenly been taken ill.

At the same moment George noticed that Josh and Luke seemed to have disappeared, and Marco was standing outside the door leading to the cockpit as if on guard, with his back to it. He was obviously making sure he kept an eye on all the young passengers in the cabin. It was all rather surprising!

George turned to look at Daniel – she thought he was much the nicest of the four couriers. The young man was chatting to one of the stewardesses. But George noticed that the stewardess seemed to have her mind on something else – and she wasn't smiling, which was unusual. Her eyes kept straying towards the loudspeaker, as if she wondered why the message had stopped coming over it. Suddenly she left Daniel, with a brief apology.

'Excuse me, please – I must go and have a word with the captain,' she told him.

George saw her making for the cockpit, but when the stewardess put out her hand to open the door Marco stopped her.

'I'm afraid you can't come in,' he said, loud enough for everyone to hear. 'Go and sit down, back there!'

Just for a moment the stewardess seemed stunned. But then she pulled herself together.

'Let me by, please!' she said firmly. 'Go and sit down yourself, sir! You are not allowed in this part of the plane. No passengers in the cockpit; it's against regulations.'

An ugly expression came over Marco's face. 'Now, don't make me lose my temper,' he said threateningly. 'Be a good girl and do as I say – or you'll be sorry!'

Anne, sitting behind George, suddenly uttered a stifled cry. Dick, Julian and George all stared in amazement!

For Marco had just taken an automatic pistol out of his pocket – and he was pointing it at the stewardess!

Chapter Two

THE HIJACKERS

'What – what on earth do you think you're doing?' gasped the stewardess.

Marco didn't bother to reply. The cockpit door behind him had just opened, and Josh appeared in the doorway. He was carrying a gun too – and now George realised what was happening.

'Hijackers!' she whispered to her cousins.

As the other passengers recovered from their first stunned surprise, they began to react. Some of them cried out in alarm, others protested indignantly or shouted angrily. Daniel jumped up from his seat as if he were about to fling himself forward.

'Are you mad?' he cried. 'Stop this stupid game of yours at once! Can't you see you're frightening the children?'

Josh strode over to him and pushed him down in his seat again.

'You keep quiet too, or it'll be the worse for you!' he told him.

Realising that this wasn't just a bad joke, Daniel did as the other young man told him. He kept quiet – it wasn't going to be any use for him to protest.

Then Josh turned to face the young passengers. Most of them were looking terrified. There was an expression of chilly determination on the courier's own face.

'Now, listen to me, young people!' he began, trying to soften his voice a bit. 'You've already guessed what's going on, haven't you?'

Dick couldn't control himself any longer. 'You're hijackers!' he cried. 'You're stealing this aircraft!'

Josh gave Dick a mocking smile – but his eyes were as cold as ever when he looked at the boy. 'That's right, young man! You've got the idea! Yes, we're hijackers – and it's up to all you kids what happens next. If all goes smoothly, nobody will be hurt. I'll explain what we plan to do soon – meanwhile, just stay where you are; carry on talking or reading or listening to music, and so long as you're sensible no harm will come to you!'

He turned to Luke, who had just come out of the cockpit too.

'Everything okay in there?' he asked his accomplice.

'Fine! The captain and his co-pilot and the radio

operator won't be giving us any more trouble, don't worry!'

Daniel started up in his seat again. 'What have you done with them?' he growled.

'You shut up!' Josh shouted at him. 'We've only trussed them up so they're helpless – we haven't hurt them!'

'At the moment the plane's on automatic pilot,' Luke went on. 'I'll take over the controls myself once I've dealt with the cabin staff here.'

He pointed to the stewards and stewardesses, standing motionless in the centre gangway and at the back of the cabin.

First of all, Luke went over to the stewardess who was standing beside Marco. He took her by the arm and made her walk in front of him. By threatening them with his pistol, he got all the cabin staff into the service areas of the plane, such as the galleys and toilets, and locked them in. Then he went back to the cockpit doorway and disappeared inside it. Marco was laughing, in a mocking way.

'Let's hope he's as good a pilot as he told us,' he said to Josh. 'Seeing that our lives are in his hands . . . and he's never piloted anything except light tourist aircraft before! A big long-haul plane like this is a different matter. I wonder if he can handle it . . .'

Josh gave him an angry look.

'Stop fooling about, Marco! You talk too much!' he snapped. 'Just bear it in mind that Luke's the brains of this outfit – if he says he can handle the plane, then he can! You'd better just shut up and stop scaring these kids!'

George never took her eyes off the hijackers. She and her cousins had been expecting exciting holidays – but things were getting rather *too* exciting! However, *she* wasn't scared. All this was interesting, to say the least of it, and the prospect of adventure made her blood run faster. That was George all over! Whatever happened, she was ready to keep on the alert and see what she could make of the situation.

Just at the moment, now the first surprise of the hijacking was over, she was watching the behaviour of 'the enemy', as she thought of the three hijackers. 'Josh is a curious sort of character,' she decided, feeling rather interested in him. He seemed to be such a big, brutal sort of man, and yet that last remark of his showed that he wasn't entirely heartless.

She turned to Anne and smiled reassuringly at her cousin. 'Don't worry, Anne,' she told her quietly. 'They won't actually eat you alive! Something tells me we're heading for a really thrilling adventure, but we'll be all right in the end. Gosh, what a story we'll have to tell when we get home!'

Anne stared at her cousin in amazement.

'George – are you *mad*?' she whispered. 'Even supposing we *do* get out of this all right, have you thought how worried our parents will be when they hear about the hijack?'

'I'm afraid Anne's right,' said Julian, looking very gloomy. 'They've put the radio operator out of action, and the control tower in Rio must already be trying to call the plane and getting no reply.'

'Yes, and a hijacking always gets into the headlines,' agreed Dick. 'Pretty soon we'll be news all over the world. Our parents *will* be worried, and no mistake!'

'Well, I'm sorry about that,' said George, but not sounding *very* sorry! 'However, there isn't anything we can do about it, is there? What *I* want to know is what our three hijacking friends are planning to do with us. Oh, if only good old Timmy was here he could go for Josh, and then we'd disarm Marco and overpower Luke, and everything would be back to normal!'

Although George really believed what she said, Julian, who was rather more down-to-earth than his cousin, had no illusions about the very real danger of their situation just now. All the passengers were at the mercy of the hijackers – and the cabin was buzzing like a beehive as the young people talked, some in an undertone, some in voices that rose sharply. A few of the younger children were sobbing and couldn't stop.

Josh's voice cut through the noise. 'Silence!' he ordered. 'Now, you are all going to keep quiet and listen to me! I repeat that I'm counting on you to do as I say, and then you'll be all right. But before I tell you exactly what I want you to do, I'll just explain that my friends and I are planning to divert this aircraft off course so as to join up with – with some friends of ours whose business is – er – getting goods into Colombia without going to the trouble of passing through Customs . . .'

'Smuggling,' Marco explained more briefly, just in case anyone didn't get the idea!

The children looked at each other, and Josh went on.

'We didn't have the money to pay for our air fares, and in any case we thought an aircraft would be a great help in our rather – well, unusual line of business, so we thought this was a risk worth taking! Luke got hold of forged papers which helped us get taken on as couriers on this holiday trip of yours: we do speak Spanish and Portuguese as well as English. So altogether, we have a good chance of succeeding – and if you children don't give us any trouble, our plan will go smoothly and won't endanger any of *you*.'

'You must be feeling very sure of yourselves, telling us all this so frankly!' said Daniel, the one courier who *wasn't* in the plot. He sounded rather angry.

'Let's just say Josh here likes to show off!' said Marco, winking at his accomplice. 'But *I* think we'll do it, too – so carry on, Josh!'

'Oh, thanks – very kind of you!' said Josh sarcastically. 'Well, for a start we'll touch down at Rio, just as the tour organisers planned.'

George and her cousins held their breath. If the plane did touch down at Rio de Janeiro, there might be a chance of getting away from the hijackers!

'But we'll only stay there long enough to refuel and take food on board,' Josh went on. 'The captain of this aircraft will be sending a message to the airport authorities himself, telling them what's up, so everything will be ready when we arrive. Now, here's the important part so far as you're concerned: we certainly don't want to be lumbered with the plane's passengers and crew, so we'll be letting you out as soon as we land.'

Once again Marco evidently thought it was up to him to add his own explanation. 'He means you've got nothing to fear from us so long as you don't make any trouble. Get it?'

There was a great sigh of relief in the cabin – obviously everybody was ready to go along with what the hijackers wanted.

Julian leaned over to whisper to George and Dick. 'They're crazy! Ten to one the police will step in once we've landed and the passengers are all out, and they'll never be able to take off again.'

'Julian, it's not going to be that easy!' George whispered back. 'Bet you anything Josh and Luke and Marco have thought of *that* one! And they'll have taken their precautions already. All I'm wondering is *what* precautions?'

She was soon to know – Josh was going on with his speech to the passengers.

'Of course we'll have to keep a hostage with us to stop the police acting and to make sure we're free to take off again. And Marco is going to pick that hostage.'

The passengers had turned pale at the mention of the word 'hostage'. Just as they'd thought they were going to be all right, here was another threat to their safety! So Marco was to pick a victim to safeguard the hijackers – and obviously they'd be taking the hostage away with them!

Julian tried to reassure the others. 'They'll pick a member of the crew, I expect – maybe they'll even pick poor Daniel, though I hope not,' he said.

Marco was now walking down the centre gangway, his bright little eyes wandering from face to anxious face. Terrified, the young people were waiting for him to make his choice.

He stepped a few paces away from George and her cousins.

'We need a really *appealing* hostage,' he

murmured. 'Somebody to touch the public's heart so the police won't dare to act. Not an adult . . . a child, definitely a child. A little girl, preferably . . .'

His glance fell upon George. She stared defiantly back.

Marco shook his head and took another step – and then he stopped right beside Anne. Terribly frightened, the little girl shrank away from him, nestling close to her big brother.

'Well, well!' said Marco. 'Just what we want! A dear little fair-haired girl! Sweet and appealing as anyone could wish for – nobody will want any harm to come to *her*!'

And he put out his hand and seized poor little Anne's wrist!

'Come along, my dear. You'll be the perfect hostage,' he said.

Anne uttered a cry of dismay, and Julian put his arm protectively round her. Dick and George both jumped up from their seats.

'You leave my sister alone!' said Julian firmly.

'Take your hands off her!' cried Dick.

'Just you wait!' said George, almost pushing her way past Dick so that she could try jumping on Marco.

As for Marco himself, he took a step backwards. 'Now then, kids – take it easy!' he said, waving his gun at them. 'None of that, or the little girl will suffer for it. You might as well be pulling the

trigger yourselves.'

George, Julian and Dick didn't really think he'd put his threat into practice . . . but how could they be sure? It was horrible, and infuriating, but they realised they'd have to do as he said.

'*That's* better!' said Marco sarcastically. 'Come along, little girl, we're on our way!' he added, pulling Anne up out of her seat.

'Look, please let her go – take me as a hostage instead!' Julian begged him.

'Or me!' said Dick.

'No, me!' said George. 'You wanted a girl, didn't you? Well, *I'm* a girl!'

You might think that was brave of George – and the suggestion was even braver, coming from her, than it was when Julian and Dick offered to be hostages. She hated being a girl so much and, what with her boyish look and her nickname of George, people very often did take her for a boy, so it cost her an effort to call herself a girl out loud! And to make matters worse, Marco didn't believe her.

'Oh, a girl, are you?' he said, sarcastically. 'Go on! You don't think you can take me in like that, do you? A girl, you? You've got a nerve!'

George went red. Meanwhile Anne was getting control of herself again. She was very pale, but she had stopped struggling.

'I don't want you to take either of my brothers, *or* my cousin Georgina,' said the brave little girl. 'I'd rather be your hostage myself!'

That was Anne all over, as the other children knew – she might seem timid, but she was full of courage when it really mattered. They all looked at her admiringly.

'Okay,' said Marco, rather gruffly – because in spite of himself, his heart had been touched for a moment. 'Okay, you come with me.'

Anne bent her head and did as he said in silence. Everyone in the cabin watched, appalled, as he took her over to the cockpit doorway and made her go through it.

'You'll find Luke in there,' he said. 'Go and sit down beside him and keep perfectly still.'

Then he closed the door and went back to stand beside Josh.

'Now, all of you listen to me!' said Josh, addressing the passengers again. 'And fasten your seatbelts, because we'll soon be landing. Don't forget what I said just now. No shouting, no pushing – you'll go down the steps one by one in good order. The crew will follow you down, and I'll be behind them with my gun to see the provisions and the fuel come on board and make sure no one tries any funny business. Marco will be watching operations from the cabin here, and Luke will stay in the cockpit with our previous hostage. The police have been informed that if they try anything, the little girl suffers for it. And that's a promise!'

Chapter Three

ANNE THE HOSTAGE

The young people all fastened their seat-belts in silence. There was no sound to be heard but the hum of the engines. Most of the passengers were too concerned with their own safety to think about poor little Anne any more. Suppose Luke crashed the plane when he brought it down? Suppose the police and the hijackers exchanged gunfire? They weren't by any means out of danger yet.

The runways and the airport buildings could already be seen down below. It was a nerve-racking moment! But at last the big plane touched down, quite gently. Figures began racing towards it from all sides, among them policemen in uniform.

The hijackers had given detailed instructions by radio transmission: no vehicles were to come anywhere near the plane. The police were to be unarmed and would only be allowed to stand by and see that the passengers and crew left in safety.

Everything went according to plan. The passengers walked from the aircraft, leaving their luggage behind in the hijackers' hands.

The crew had been let out of their 'cells', and followed the passengers: first the stewardesses and then the stewards. Josh was the last to come down the ramp, holding his pistol. Marco was keeping watch up in the plane itself, with a sub-machine gun, but he knew he and his friends had nothing to fear from the police. Anne, as their hostage, was a guarantee that *they* would be safe enough!

Poor little Anne — time seemed to her to be passing so slowly. It was like a nightmare. She sat in the cockpit beside Luke, thinking that she had never been in a situation as bad as this before. She had often been in all kinds of danger, because the Five had had many adventures which meant running risks — but at least she'd had George and her brothers with her then. Now, however, she was all on her own in the hands of the hijackers. She knew they wouldn't shrink from anything if they were in a tight spot . . . Big tears rose to her eyes and trickled down her cheeks.

Suddenly, much to her surprise, someone tapped her gently on the shoulder, and she heard a voice in her ear.

'Don't cry, Anne,' it said. 'You've nothing to

fear with me, and you'll be free again in a few days' time!'

It was Luke! The young hijacker was actually smiling at her.

'We're not inhuman, you know!' he said, sighing. 'We may not be exactly law-abiding, and yes, we *do* smuggle goods – but as I said, we really aren't inhuman!'

Anne's tears dried up at once. She was a clever and sensitive little girl, and she could tell that Luke wasn't as bad as his friends. Suddenly she felt sorry for him, being part of this gang of smugglers.

'Wh – why do you do it?' she said hesitantly. It wasn't a very clear way of putting her question, but Luke seemed to understand what she meant.

'You mean why did I let myself in for this sort of thing?' he said quietly. 'Well – if you once go wrong it's hard to get back on the straight and narrow path! I used to be an instructor at a private aviation club, and one day I stupidly took some of the petty cash. After that I somehow never had the courage to retrace my steps. I wish I *had* gone straight, but it's too late now. I can't let Josh and Marco down.'

'Oh no, it isn't too late – I mean, it's *never* too late to do the *right* thing!' said Anne in her gentle little voice. 'And if you weren't a hijacker and a smuggler, I – I'd like you very much!' she added with her usual honesty.

Luke smiled, but he didn't reply. Instead, he leaned towards the window to see what was happening outside the plane.

'We'll be taking off again soon,' he said a moment later. 'I hope I can pilot this plane as far as the Amazon – that's where we're going to land, on a makeshift runway,' he added after a short pause. 'Our friends are waiting for us in a spot nearby. Marco will operate the radio for me, and I think it will be all right.'

Anne shivered. She felt as if she were all alone in the world. Any moment now the plane would be leaving Rio, and she would be flying away from Julian, Dick and George. All of a sudden she remembered Timmy.

'Oh, I hope the hijackers haven't put him out of the plane too,' she thought to herself. 'If he's still here I can get *him* back, for company – I'd feel braver with dear old Timmy. He's such a good, strong, intelligent, loving dog! He'd defend me if I needed it, too.'

Everyone was still very busy on the airfield out-side. The policemen were watching, furious but powerless to do anything about it, as workmen finished refuelling the plane. The crew and passengers had already disappeared in the direction of the airport buildings, with a whole crowd of newspaper reporters round them.

Looking over Luke's shoulder, Anne saw them

go. Her brothers and her cousin must be among the crowd – when would she see them again?

Josh soon came into the cockpit, followed by Marco.

'Ready, Luke? They're all standing by to watch us leave down there – so off you go, old fellow!'

It seemed ages before the plane really took off from the runway, and Anne's heart was thudding with alarm. Once off the ground, the aircraft gained height. When Luke said they were flying at an altitude of twelve thousand metres and a speed of a thousand kilometres an hour, Josh and Marco relaxed.

'Done it!' said Marco, triumphantly. 'We've got safe away! And thanks to little Anne here, nobody will dare follow us.'

Josh turned to Anne. 'You can walk round the plane if you like,' he told her. 'We don't mean you any harm, remember!'

He opened the door into the cabin for her, pushed her out into the central gangway of the cabin, and followed her out himself – and then a cry of amazement from the little girl made him look round.

'Julian! Dick! George!' cried Anne, quite beside herself with joy, and she dashed forward.

Josh could hardly believe his eyes. George and her two boy cousins had just appeared from behind the seats where they had been hiding. They looked very pleased with themselves.

'What do you think you're doing here?' said Josh, staggered. 'Why did you hide in the cabin? I never even thought of *counting* the passengers getting out. I was sure they'd all be in a great hurry to leave the plane!'

'Not us!' said George, rather scornfully. 'You didn't think we'd just leave Anne in your hands, did you? The four of us and my dog are the Five, and the Five are *never* separated! We'll take on anyone you like!'

This grand speech didn't impress Josh much – after all, he didn't know the Famous Five!

'Well, that's your bad luck!' he growled. 'We've got four hostages instead of one – who knows, that may be a good idea!'

Shaking his head, he went off to tell Luke and Marco the news, while Anne hugged her brothers and her cousin. They were all delighted to be together again – you'd have thought they were being reunited after a long, long time away from each other. Anne was shedding tears of joy.

'Oh, I'm *so* happy!' she said. 'You didn't go after all – you didn't leave me behind!'

'As if we would!' said Julian.

'Honestly, Anne, would we do a thing like that?' Dick asked her.

'We can defend ourselves *much* better when we're all five together,' added George – who hadn't forgotten about her dear Timmy.

The next few hours didn't feel quite real. Josh, doing the job of cook and steward, gave everyone on board a meal on a tray, but he was so clumsy about it that Anne, laughing, offered to help him. He accepted her help with rather a bad grace. Luke smiled at Anne as she brought him his own share of the meal.

'Thanks – I must keep my strength up,' he said. 'It will soon be dark, and I'll need to be very much on the alert to pilot this plane. It's not exactly easy.'

'Oh, you'll do it okay,' said Marco confidently.

'The main thing is to keep going for the next few hours,' said Josh, 'and then we'll be in radio contact with our friends. They can give us the directions we'll need for landing.'

'And when will you be letting *us* go?' asked Julian. 'It won't be all that simple to find some inhabited place where you can leave us!'

'Don't worry,' said Marco. 'One of our friends will take you to a Mission we know in the forest, and then the missionaries will see you get back to civilisation again.'

It didn't sound very reassuring, but the children had to be content with that. However, they were beginning to feel rather downhearted, and when night fell George suggested, 'We'd better try to get some sleep. Then we might feel better.'

The four of them lay down on the seats of the

plane cabin and went to sleep, but George kept having nightmares. She had asked Josh to let Timmy out of his compartment, but it was no good. Josh, who didn't like dogs, said no. Just now, however, Josh was asleep himself and snoring – he wasn't much of a guard, but then there was nothing much the children could have done to the hijackers, with the plane so high in the air! Waking up yet again, George rose soundlessly and made her way towards the back of the cabin.

'If I open all the doors I *must* find the one to the compartment where animals travel,' she told herself.

And a moment later she was successful! Timmy, who was the only animal on board, had heard her coming. He began whining softly with pleasure. George untied him, knelt down beside him and talked to him just as if he were human.

'Poor old Tim!' she said softly. 'We're in a nice mess now! The Five may be used to getting out of tight spots, but this must be one of the tightest ever! We usually have a mystery to solve, too, but not this time – this is just an adventure pure and simple, without any mystery to be cleared up.'

'Woof,' agreed Timmy helpfully, wagging his tail. 'Woof, woof!' George looked at him as if he'd replied in human language.

'You're quite right!' she told him. 'Adventures mean action, so we must *do* something! As soon as we land I'll try and find some way to give the hijackers the slip.'

George went back to her seat in the cabin, followed by Timmy – but she hadn't quite reached it when the plane suddenly jolted, making her lose her balance. She clutched at the back of her seat.

'What's happening?' she gasped.

Josh woke and jumped up. Julian, Dick and Anne had been shaken awake too, and they exchanged glances of inquiry. The plane shook in the air again – it was a bit like a horse bucking. Josh ran to the cockpit, followed by the children. Marco had left his place by the radio equipment, and was standing next to Luke. Luke himself seemed to be having difficulty with the controls.

'What's happening?' Josh asked, echoing George.

Luke did not even look round. At that moment the plane bucked again, violently, and then levelled out.

'Can't make it out!' said Luke, through his gritted teeth. 'This wretched –'

But another even more violent jolt interrupted him. He tried to right the aircraft once more, but it was beginning to lose speed. 'There's something wrong,' Luke told him. 'And I don't think it's anything *I* did wrong, either.'

Josh and Marco looked at him, obviously worried. The Five – including Timmy, who could

tell by instinct that something unusual was up – stood clustered together behind him. They were all holding their breath.

'Luke, we're not going to fall out of the sky, are we?' asked Marco, his voice thin with alarm. 'You'll get us out of this, okay?'

'The controls aren't responding properly – and it's getting worse,' said Luke. He didn't sound at all happy about things! 'I can't work miracles, you know.'

And now the plane seemed to be nose-diving down towards the ground in almost total darkness. They were in a desperate situation!

Julian, Dick, George and Anne didn't say anything. They had gone very pale as they waited for what looked like the inevitable crash. Instinctively, the two boys had taken one of Anne's hands each, and they were all holding on to each other very tight. George was pressing her leg against Timmy's nice warm side. Luke was leaning over the controls. Josh and Marco, horrified, kept quiet.

Several seconds passed – it seemed a very long time indeed! At last Luke spoke again. 'Go and sit down and put your seat-belts on,' he told them. 'I'm going to have to try a crash landing. But I'm afraid we're flying over forest at the moment.'

He didn't need to say any more. They all realised that if they were flying over forest there wasn't much hope.

'Cheer up!' said George bravely, fastening her seat-belt. 'We've got out of trouble before!'

But all the same, she was thinking of her mother and father at home in Kirrin, and she could hardly keep back her tears.

In the cabin, Luke was doing all he could. Eyes on the altimeter, he managed to straighten the plane out again, so that at least it wasn't diving so fast. But they were still going lower and lower. If there were trees down below . . . Of course, they might be lucky enough to be over a plateau, but there was no visibility, so he couldn't tell. Luke began landing manoeuvres, anyway.

'Here goes!' he muttered to himself as he began the final part of the manoeuvre.

What happened next felt like a nightmare to the people in the plane. There was a sudden awful shock, tightening everyone's seat-belts quite painfully round them. The whole plane turned over, bounced back upright, and went round in a semi-circle, all with a frightful noise of rending metal. At last it came to a halt with its tail in the air.

Nobody moved at all for several moments. George was the first to get her wits together again. She had been holding Timmy in her arms to protect him, and he licked her face all over, barking quietly. 'Wuff, wuff!'

'Oh, darling Timmy – are you all right?' she asked. She felt terribly weak with shock and relief.

Hands trembling, she undid her seat-belt. Every-thing was dark around her – the lights of the plane had gone out. Where were her cousins? Suddenly she heard Dick, quite close to her.

'Phew! Not exactly a joy-ride!' he said.

'Dick, are you okay?' George asked anxiously.

'Yes – how about you?'

'I'm all right – what about Anne and Julian?'

Groping about in the dark, the Five soon found each other. They all had bruises, but none of them was really hurt. They heard the voices of Josh and Marco, too. It sounded as if they'd escaped injury as well. But what about Luke?

His two accomplices went into the cockpit. Luke was slumped over the controls, unconscious. Muttering to himself, Josh found a torch and switched it on. 'His forehead's bleeding,' he said out loud. 'Must have had a nasty bump – ah, he's coming round!'

Luke opened his eyes, put his hand to his head, realised that the plane wasn't moving, and managed to smile. 'I did it, then!' he said.

'You did it, Luke – you're terrific!' said Julian. 'But won't the plane catch fire?'

'Not now. It's just luck it didn't explode when we came down so suddenly!'

'Let's get out of here, anyway!' suggested George impatiently.

'Take it easy, young man – sorry, I mean young

woman!' said Luke. 'It's pitch dark, and we've no idea what dangers there may be outside. Better stay in here resting until dawn. Then I'll take our bearings to find out where we are, and we'll try to make our way to safety, even if we can't use the plane.'

Luke's suggestion was obviously a sensible one. Anne went to find the first-aid kit carried on board, and put a dressing on the pilot's injured forehead. Then they all lay down on the seats and tried to get some rest. It wasn't easy after what they'd just been through during the crash landing. The children didn't think they'd get a wink – but they did fall asleep all the same, almost at once, and it did them good.

It was broad daylight when George woke up. Her cousins were still asleep, but Josh, Luke and Marco had disappeared. Furious remarks from near the radio transmitter, however, told her that it was out of order and Marco must be trying in vain to put it right.

'Not a squeak out of the wretched thing – *now* what are we going to do?' he was grumbling.

At this moment Josh and Luke appeared. They seemed to have been out exploring their surroundings – and they were looking very glum.

Julian, Dick and Anne woke up too. George glanced inquiringly at the two men, and Luke explained the situation to everyone.

'As luck would have it, we came down on the light soil of a piece of moorland – but though that's what saved our lives, it's in the middle of virgin forest! I've taken our bearings, and we're some way from the Colombian border, near the Yapura, one of the tributaries of the Amazon. But I'm afraid we're a long way from civilisation. How about the radio, Marco? Is it working yet?'

'No, and it won't either. We're in a very tight spot indeed – and I'm not at all sure we're going to get out of it!' said Marco.

Josh, with his usual surly expression, said, 'There's a kind of hill not far off. I'll climb that, and see what I can see from the top of it. Then we'll decide what to do next.'

'I'll come with you,' said Luke.

'Can we come too?' asked George eagerly. 'We could do with stretching our legs.'

Josh shrugged his shoulders. 'Why not, if you want to?' he said.

So the children followed the two hijackers out of the plane, leaving Marco tinkering with the radio.

Chapter Four

THE RIVER

A really breathtaking sight met the children's eyes. They were surrounded by huge trees, with such thick foliage that it partly cut off the rays of the sun. The ground underfoot was soft and rather marshy, so that they had to go carefully if they didn't want to sink in. After a while it got firmer underfoot.

The hill Josh had seen was a slope that rose above the level of the treetops. It was quite rocky, like a miniature mountain, but even Timmy was able to climb it quite easily. When the children and the hijackers had arrived on the level platform made by the natural shape of the rock at the top of the slope, they couldn't help letting out cries of amazement. Down below, almost at their feet, the river Yapura flowed eastward between two wide banks of fine sand which looked bright yellow in the sunlight. About three kilometres away, the river disappeared among tall rocks, and beyond them lay the great mountain range of the Andes.

When the children could manage to tear their eyes away, they all looked at each other – they didn't need to say a word. For as far as they could see, there wasn't a single sign of civilisation. No sign of life at all, in fact! The hijackers and the Five were lost in the middle of an enormous stretch of wild countryside. Josh summed it all up.

'Well, looks as if we're in a nice mess here! And no way to get out of it, either. No radio to put out an SOS! Our provisions won't last all that long – it would be bad enough for three determined men on their own, but if we've got to lumber ourselves with a bunch of kids we might as well give up all hope of getting out of here, straight away!'

And he looked darkly at the children. They shivered! Was he thinking of leaving them to starve to death here on their own?

Luke guessed what they were thinking, and he said at once, 'Don't worry, we won't abandon you! We're all in the same situation, so we'd better work as a team. Let's think of ourselves as explorers discovering virgin territory!'

He smiled, but his eyes showed how anxious he really felt. The outlook wasn't good for the seven of them – or eight of them, counting Timmy! – whether they stayed together or not. Slowly and in silence, they all went down the hill again. The hot, humid air of the forest down below seemed stifling. They shivered as they thought of the dangers that were probably lurking among those dark leaves.

When they got back to the aircraft they found Marco looking very discouraged. He ran his fingers through his hair and admitted that he was defeated.

'There's nothing to be done about it!' he sighed. 'I'd have to spend days on end working on that wretched set to get it to work at all. I rather think we'd be dead before I got it going again!'

'Come along, we mustn't despair,' said Luke. 'We'll get ourselves organised, and you'll end up with enough power to broadcast an SOS signal. I'm sure of that. We mustn't give up so easily!'

All of a sudden it was turning out that Luke was a really good leader.

'We'll use the plane as shelter while we explore our immediate surroundings thoroughly,' he added.

'But what about food?' said Dick – who always had an excellent appetite! 'If we spend too long just exploring round here, we'll run out of provisions quite soon.'

'Dick's right,' said Julian. 'I read a travel book about the South American forests, and it said that there isn't much game in them, and lots of people have starved to death having got lost in the jungle.'

'Yes, you've got a good point there,' agreed the young pilot. 'But you're forgetting one thing: our only real chance of getting out of here is being able to send an SOS message, and at the moment the radio's out of order. We have to give Marco time to repair it.'

'I see!' said George. 'It's not much of a choice, is it? Either we set off not knowing just where to go – or we stay here and trust Marco to repair the radio.'

'Yes, and so it's a better idea to stay here.'

Once that was decided, they set about organising their day-to-day lives. They took stock of their provisions, and Luke worked out everyone's rations exactly. They were going to have to be particularly careful of water.

'What happens when we run out?' asked Josh.

George knew the answer to that! 'The river Yapura runs quite close to here – if we boil the water it'll be all right to drink. If you ask me, the problem of catching game is much more worrying.'

That was true. Apart from their pistols and a sub-machine gun – which hadn't got any extra ammunition anyway – the hijackers had no weapons. And they weren't much good at setting traps, even if there *had* been any game about.

Marco set to work again as hard as he could, to try repairing the radio, but unfortunately it had suffered a lot of damage when the plane crash-landed. There were some parts of the set which he could replace, but he had to improvise spares for other parts. Marco was a clever technician, but he just didn't have the material he needed; that was the trouble.

After several days, he told them it was no good. 'I'll never do it,' he said. 'The transmitter still won't work!'

'And provisions are running low,' said Josh gloomily. 'You'll have to do something, Luke – you're the brains of this outfit! You'd better think of a way to get us out of here, and fast, or we'll be done for! Isn't that right, Marco? Well, isn't it, you kids?'

They all agreed in their hearts. Yes, something *did* have to be done! The question was, what? Since the hijackers couldn't get in touch with their smuggler friends or indeed with anyone else by radio, there was only one thing for it now: they'd have to plunge into the forest and hope to rescue themselves that way. It was rather a forlorn hope, but they had no choice.

Luke decided to take as much as they could possibly carry in the way of food, the first-aid kit, blankets, and basic pots and pans for cooking. When he had divided the load up between himself and his friends and the children, he gave the word for them all to start off.

The children felt quite sad about leaving the

plane which had been their home for the last few days! It had been the scene of one of the most exciting adventures even *they* had ever had, as well. And now they were setting out on a new adventure, possibly even *more* exciting. How would it all end? The four cousins had taken the whole situation very bravely so far. Anne had been helping George and Josh to cook meals while the boys went out into the forest with Luke looking for game, though they never found much. Those few days spent with the hijackers had made them more like friends than prisoners and their jailers – but now they were *all* prisoners of the forest! As they left the plane behind them, George was thinking to herself, 'It's about time some luck came our way. We *will* get back to civilisation – we *must*!'

And George, who never gave up however bad things seemed, felt a little better!

The eight of them made their way, with some difficulty, through the tall, thick vegetation. Soon they reached the banks of the Yapura, and Luke suggested following the course of the river.

'We can be sure we'll always have water to drink then,' he said, 'and most important of all, we won't get lost. And if we *have* got any chance of finding an inhabited place it's most likely to be beside a river.'

The 'explorers' went on their way in the burning sun for quite a long time. The trees didn't give much shelter from the sun's hot rays on the sandy

banks of the river. Anne was beginning to feel very tired. Julian noticed, and without saying anything he took part of the load she was carrying and added it to his own.

George gritted her teeth. Poor Timmy's tongue was hanging out. Dick walked behind his cousin in silence. Josh, noticing that Anne was limping slightly, grumbled, 'These kids are going to slow us down!'

However, Luke turned round to smile at the little girl.

'Come on, Anne! We must keep going as fast as we can – but when you really get too tired to walk any more I'll carry you,' he promised.

As the sun rose higher the heat got worse, and at mid-day they stopped to eat something and bathe in the river before they went on again.

The afternoon was a real test of endurance for the children and Timmy. Luke and Marco made a kind of stretcher out of a couple of branches threaded through the sleeves of their jackets, and they carried Anne in it – the poor little girl simply couldn't walk any farther. George felt her own muscles aching with weariness. She kept looking all around her at the river, the banks and the forest. She would have given a good deal to see any sign of life at all, but she couldn't see or hear anything. Silence weighed down heavily on the little party. There was something really rather frightening about such a total absence of all life, even animal life.

Night fell quite suddenly, as it always does in the tropics. It took even Luke by surprise.

'Stop!' he said. 'We'll camp here for the night.'

The day had been boiling hot, but the night was going to be cold. Josh lit a fire, with some difficulty. He had to use green wood, which didn't burn very well and made a lot of smoke. A swarm of mosquitoes came to attack the 'explorers'.

Sitting gloomily round their camp fire, they ate their evening meal. Julian tried to keep up the spirits of the rest of the party by joking. 'When I'm a great-great-grandfather,' he said, 'I'll have a marvellous story to tell my great-great-grand-children. Just wait till they hear about *this*!'

'Oh, come off it, Ju!' said Dick. 'It's not much of a story at all! I mean, there's nothing *happening* in it – you won't even be able to tell them you were attacked by Indians. There *aren't* any Indians or anyone else at all in this deserted spot!'

'Don't you be so sure!' grunted Josh, from the place where he was sitting. 'There are Indians in these forests all right. They may not be the sort you see in films, but they're pretty tough customers all the same.'

'Are there any in these parts?' asked Anne in alarm.

'You bet there are! We can't be far from Jivaro

territory here,' said Josh.

'Jivaro?' asked George.

'The Jivaros are a very fierce tribe – they shrink human heads! And if they happened to get wind of *us* in these parts, they'd be after us in no time. That'd be the end of us, you can be sure!' said Josh.

'That's enough of that, Josh,' said Luke firmly. 'Stop scaring the children can't you?'

Josh laughed and said no more. Meanwhile, Marco was undoing the blankets.

'Let's roll ourselves up in these and get some sleep,' he suggested.

'Wait a minute!' Luke interrupted him. 'We ought to have somebody on guard. We'll take it in turns – one keeps watch while the rest of us sleep. You take the first watch, Marco. Wake me up at midnight. I'll take the second watch, and then Josh can take the third one.'

The children were worn out. They fell asleep at once, nestling close to each other, and faithful old Timmy snuggled up beside George. Even in the South American jungle, Timmy was a wonderful comfort! Silence reigned, broken only by the crackle of sparks from the fire as Marco put more wood on it.

He was supposed to be keeping watch – but he soon felt sleepy himself. He closed his eyes, telling himself he'd just rest for five minutes and then he'd be on the alert again. But of course he wasn't – he too fell asleep, instead.

George never knew just what it was that woke her. A tiny sound out in the forest, perhaps. She opened her eyes – and so did Timmy, of course – and saw Marco lying there asleep in the light of the dying fire. Feeling anxious, she sat up, ready to shake him awake again. And it was then that an inferno seemed to break loose all around them!

A band of Indians armed with spears and a few old guns rushed out of the trees, yelling ferociously, and surrounded the bewildered little party. The 'explorers' soon found they were powerless. A dozen Indian warriors got to work tying them up with jungle creepers lashed around their chests and arms, so that they couldn't even move their hands.

'The Jivaros!' whispered the terrified Josh.

Chapter Five

THE JIVAROS

Brave as they all were, the children had never felt so scared in their lives. But Timmy wasn't scared, not he! Seeing somebody attacking his little mistress, he was about to leap at the Indian's throat, but George stopped him.

'No, Tim! Don't!' she cried. 'Leave it! Good dog!'

She was afraid the Indians would kill her beloved Timmy before her very eyes, and that would be more than she could bear! Dear old Timmy obeyed, even if he didn't understand. The Jivaros stood there grinning broadly at their prisoners. They seemed very pleased with themselves, and were chattering away to each other in their own language.

They wore nothing except skirts made out of creepers dyed red and yellow, and fringed anklets and armlets of the same material. One of them was wearing two long feathers in his hair. He seemed to be their leader. Luke looked this man in the eye and asked, 'What do you want?'

Of course, the Indian didn't understand the words, but he obviously got the idea behind them because he pointed to the forest and uttered a string of words in his own language before he and his men made their prisoners walk on with them through the trees.

The Indians were carrying lighted torches, so they could see their way. 'Do you think they're taking us to their chief?' whispered George to Anne.

'And what exactly do you suppose they'll do with us?' grunted Marco. He was furious with himself. 'If only I hadn't dropped off to sleep!'

'I don't think that'd really have made much difference,' Julian said. 'The Indians easily out-number us – and they're at least as well armed as we are.'

Surrounded by the Jivaros, the party of captives made its way along a narrow path winding through the trees. Poor little Anne felt she'd been walking for about a hundred years when they came out at last in a clearing. It was full of huts made out of branches, and was obviously the Jivaros' village. There was one hut in the middle which was bigger than the others. The Indians and their prisoners went towards it. A huge Indian wearing toucan feathers in his hair appeared in the doorway. He was obviously the chief!

George and her companions were pushed towards him.

The chief, a man in the prime of life, looked very surprised when he saw the children. He stared at them in silence for a long time, and then barked out a series of brief orders. One group of Jivaros immediately seized George and her cousins, and another group took hold of the hijackers. They all thought their last hour had come.

However, it hadn't! The Indians only led them off and shut them up in two empty huts, one for the children and one for the adults. Faithful old Timmy had followed George, of course.

When the Five were on their own again inside the hut, which was dimly lit by a couple of burning torches, they looked at each other in dismay.

'Well!' said Dick. 'We certainly *are* having an interesting time — too interesting by half! We thought we were off for an exciting holiday, but we didn't expect *this* sort of thing. It could hardly be worse — it's just one awful thing happening after another! First a hijacked plane, then a crash landing in the middle of the jungle, and now here we are in the hands of the head-hunters!'

'Do — do you really think they're going to cut off *our* heads and shrink them?' whispered Anne.

'No, of course not, Anne!' said Julian in a brisk, comforting voice. 'There aren't any real head-hunters left these days. Even if the Jivaro Indians do still shrink heads, they'll be the heads of people who've already died, so don't worry!'

'Julian's right,' said Dick. 'I saw a shrunken head in a museum once, and it was very old. I must say it didn't look what you might call pretty – they sort of dry the heads, and they keep their features but the skull-bones have been removed, though the hair stays on, and the result is most peculiar. I wouldn't like *my* head to be –'

'Oh, for goodness' sake, *shut up*, Dick!' George interrupted him. Like Julian, she didn't want him to scare timid Anne. 'We've got to do something, and pretty quick too! Let's try and think of a way to get out of here. If we could manage to get back to the wrecked plane we'd have shelter of a kind. But we'd need Luke and the others to escape with us. We can't get very far without them.'

Julian agreed. Resourceful as they might be, the Five would stand very little chance in the forest alone. Come to that, they didn't stand much chance even with Luke, Josh and Marco, but anything was better than staying in the hands of the Jivaro Indians.

'And even if we don't manage to escape, at least it'll give us hope and something to occupy our minds,' thought Julian, with his usual common sense. 'Yes,' he added out loud. 'Let's try and think how to get away. For a start, we need to get in touch with the others again.'

George and Dick were already searching every corner of the hut. Their prison was made of stout branches lashed together with strong creepers. The children had no knife, so it was no use thinking of cutting the creepers and making a hole in the wall of the hut like that.

The mud floor was very hard, too, so there was no chance of digging a tunnel.

George turned to the door, which was fastened by a rough sort of latch. She tried this latch, not very hopefully, and was surprised to find that the door was not fastened on the outside. She'd expected there would be a bar of wood or something like that fixed across it, to stop the captives opening it from the inside, but she couldn't feel any resistance as she pushed the door.

Taking all sorts of precautions, the brave girl opened it until she could see through the crack. Outside, the children saw the clearing, with fires burning in front of the huts.

Slowly and carefully, George opened the door even further. She was just about to slip through the crack herself when a shadowy figure suddenly appeared in front of her.

A Jivaro warrior was looking at her – he didn't seem fierce, but it was obvious what he meant!

George hastily retreated back into the hut. The man on guard outside didn't even bother to close the door after her.

'So that's no good!' said Dick gloomily, feeling very disappointed. 'We might have known they'd post guards to stop us getting away.'

By now Timmy had had enough of the hut. He didn't think it smelt very nice, and he wanted some fresh air. Since the door was still open, he went through it and explored the clearing round the hut, wagging his tail. The Indian guard didn't take any notice of him. Obviously his instructions to see the children didn't get away did not apply to animals too.

That gave George an idea.

'Listen!' she whispered. 'I've thought of something! We can use Timmy to get in touch wth Luke and the others.'

'How do you mean?' asked Julian, not very hopefully.

'Easy, Ju! I'll write a short message and tie it to Timmy's collar!'

'A short message saying what?'

'Saying we've got to risk an escape!' George explained. 'I don't suppose the hut where they've put Luke and co. is fastened on the outside, any more than ours is. Haven't you noticed how quiet everything is? The Jivaros must have gone off to sleep feeling quite happy now they've caught us! All except for the two warriors on guard outside. Well, if each group attacks its own guard at the same moment, we'll have the advantage of surprise — and then we can get away together. That's what I'm going to suggest!'

'It sounds awfully risky to me, George,' said Julian doubtfully.

'Nothing ventured, nothing gained!' George reminded him.

Julian still didn't see how the Five could possibly overpower their guard and silence him before he had a chance to alert the rest of the tribe. However, they might as well find out what Luke thought of George's idea!

When she had written her note in the light of the torches, she whistled quietly to call Timmy. The good dog appeared in the hut again at once. George tied the message to his collar.

'Find Luke, Timmy!' she told him. 'Luke — remember Luke?' And she pointed to the doorway.

Timmy understood at once. He shot off through the dark towards the hut where the other three captives were imprisoned, and a moment later George saw him coming back as fast as he had gone — with another note: a short answer from Luke.

'Don't do anything silly,' the young man had written. 'And whatever you do, don't move. We think we've found a way to escape. Send Timmy back in about an hour.'

George resigned herself to waiting. That hour seemed a very long one – all the longer because it was obviously going to get light soon, and then it would be much more difficult to escape! At last the time came for her to send Timmy back to Luke again. This time the message he brought back with him was one that stunned the children!

'The three of us are going,' Luke had written. 'We're not taking you – it would slow us down and give us less chance of finding our way to safety, but don't worry, we won't forget you! We'll be back with help as soon as we can – always supposing we survive ourselves. Don't lose heart!'

'Oh no!' cried Dick. 'Leaving us in the lurch! How *could* they?'

Julian was staggered too, and felt too discouraged to say anything! Even George was at a loss for words, she was so upset. It was left to Anne, of all people, to encourage her brothers and her cousin.

'I'm sure Luke means what he says,' she told them in her soft little voice. 'He won't just abandon us. We must trust him!'

So now there was nothing the children could do but wait – and it was a very tense wait, too. They were all on the alert, listening for any noise outside. But time went by and nothing happened. Had Luke, Josh and Marco decided not to try escaping after all? Or had they already got away somehow without making any noise?

There was no way at all for the Five to find out!

At last the sky grew pale. Dawn was coming, and the Indians lit fires. Some of them began to move around the clearing. Their daily round was beginning. Suddenly the door of the children's hut was opened. A woman came in with a woven basket full of fruit. She put it down in front of the children without a word.

'Come on, breakfast!' said Julian. 'What wouldn't I give for a nice plate of eggs and bacon? Still, this fruit looks quite nice.'

But at that moment they heard a voice shouting not far away – a woman's voice, calling something out hoarsely. The children saw Jivaros running past the open door of their hut. There was a lot of shouting, and in a moment the whole village was in uproar!

'So now we know!' said Dick, looking a bit pale. 'Luke and the others *have* got away – and the woman taking them breakfast has just discovered they're not there. The Jivaros must be furious! Let's hope they aren't going to take it out on *us*!'

Chapter Six

THE WITCH DOCTOR

The children dared not open the door of their hut any more, but they peered through the crack. They saw a party of Jivaro warriors set off into the forest. Obviously they were in pursuit of Luke, Josh and Marco. Would they catch up with the three men?

It was broad daylight now, and soon the shouting of the Jivaro warriors faded away in the distance. However, the village was still very busy. Nobody came to see the children, and George and her cousins began to feel they could breathe a little more easily.

The woman who had brought them breakfast and then found that Luke and his friends had gone must have said that the children, at least, were still there. And no reasonable person could think they were responsible for the hijackers' escape! On the other hand, *were* the Jivaros reasonable people? They'd soon find out!

George sighed heavily. 'Honestly, I think the worst part is having to wait!'

But she didn't have to wait much longer for something to happen. At that moment their Jivaro guard came in. They couldn't tell anything from his face. He made signs telling them to get up, and then pointed to the door. There was no mistaking what *that* meant – the Five stood up and hurried out of the hut. Following the Indian, they went over the clearing in the direction of the chief's hut.

However, their guard led them to another hut instead, almost as big as the chief's hut but farther away. The children were only about ten paces away from it when a very strange figure came out – they almost cried out in surprise!

George had never seen anything so extraordinary in her life! The man who stood there in front of them was taller than most of the Indians, and his face was covered with a terrifying mask crowned with feathers and big plumes. He wore an amazing costume made of animal skins, wild beasts' teeth, feathers and brightly coloured tassels. George knew that in some savage tribes, witch doctors dressed up in ceremonial robes for important occasions – was it possible that this one was going to sacrifice the Indians' prisoners to one of their cruel gods?

The man looked at them for a long time, in silence, and then he put his hand on Julian's head. There didn't seem anything particularly threatening about that. He did the same with Dick, George, and Anne, whereupon the Jivaro guard turned round and walked off. The Five were left alone with the witch doctor. They realised that this strange being had taken them under his wing and shown that he'd protect them. But they still didn't feel very happy about it!

Now the witch doctor was pointing to his hut, signing to them to go in. George turned round and saw a big crowd of Indians, men, women and children, standing not far away and watching intently. The witch doctor turned to the crowd too and made gestures which obviously meant that the prisoners were his.

Dick tried to make a joke. 'Will you come into my parlour, said the spider to the fly?' he muttered, looking at the witch doctor. 'Oh, what big *teeth* you've got, Grandpa!' he added, as he glanced at the teeth on the witch doctor's robes.'All the better to eat you with, I suppose!'

'Shut up, you ass!' Julian told his brother, quite crossly. 'You're only making matters worse!'

Inside, the witch doctor's hut looked as extraordinary as its owner. There were all sorts of masks hanging from the walls – along with the shrunken heads that were part of the Jivaros' traditional

71

ceremonies.

'Gosh – this is like being in an adventure film!' thought George. 'If only it *were* a film, and not real!'

But she couldn't shake off the feeling that there *was* something unreal abut the hut. Like the witch doctor himself, it seemed just a bit larger than life, like a stage set!

There were two Jivaro women in the hut, and when the witch doctor gave them an order they went over to the children, daubed their cheeks with red and yellow paint, and then made them each put on a kind of waistcoat, also in red and yellow. After that the witch doctor pushed the children out of his hut again and showed them to the people who were gathered there.

The crowd murmured with satisfaction at the sight of their captives in this weird get-up. Then the witch doctor went back into his hut and the Jivaros all went about their usual business. To the children's great surprise, they were left alone with Timmy.

'Well, *I* don't know!' said Julian, baffled. 'I can't make head or tail of this!'

'We seem to be free!' suggested Anne timidly.

'I don't suppose it's as easy as that,' said George. 'There must be some reason for this little ceremony we've just performed.'

'Let's get these stupid things off and go and

wash our faces!' said Dick, starting to take his waistcoat off.

'Hold on!' George warned him. 'I've an idea these clothes and the paint are a kind of passport – let's try walking around the place and see what happens.'

The children walked slowly towards the last of the village huts, which stood near the forest. As they passed, the Indians looked at them without showing any hostility. But when they actually reached the forest path, a warrior stood before them, barring the way, and they had to turn back.

They tried again in several other places, with no better success. It didn't take them long to work out that they were allowed to move freely in the village itself, but they were not to leave it.

'Oh well!' said Julian philosophically. 'At least we've got *some* freedom of movement. Perhaps that'll help us find some way to escape.'

The Five soon adjusted to their new life. They ate and slept in the same hut as before, but they could spend the rest of the time as they pleased, so long as they wore their red and yellow waistcoats.

When they had been in the village for forty-eight hours, the chief, Pfo, sent for them. The witch doctor led the children to Pfo's big hut, and once they were there he put his hand on their heads and spoke earnestly to the chief. He seemed to agree. George noticed that the witch doctor, whose name

73

was Rna, obviously had a lot of influence over the chief, and since Rna seemed well disposed towards the Five she was very glad of that!

One evening, when the Five were alone in their hut, she asked her cousins, 'I say – don't you think there's something odd about Rna?'

'*Something* odd?' said Dick. 'He's about the oddest person I've ever met, in *every* way!'

'No, what I mean is, he's not at all like the other Jivaros,' George explained.

'Yes, you're right,' Anne agreed.

'Well, I suppose all witch doctors have to stand apart from the common people,' said Dick. 'A little bit of mystery won't do him any harm with them! He's probably worth about ten totems at a go!'

'No, seriously!' George persisted. 'He does make a very funny impression on me. Like a witch doctor out of a play! The other Jivaros seem quite ordinary by comparison, except when they've got their war paint on.'

'Like the warriors who set off after Luke and Josh and Marco,' said Dick. 'Not that it helped them much!'

That was true – the party who had gone in pursuit of the hijackers had come back empty-handed and disappointed. George just hoped Luke and his friends would get back to civilisation very soon!

'What I'm driving at,' she went on, 'is that the

74

Jivaros are simple people at heart, but I don't think their witch doctor is, not at all. And why doesn't he ever take his mask off in public?'

'Perhaps he's hideously ugly?' suggested Dick. 'Or maybe he has some nasty skin disease – or he just doesn't like the air on his face!'

'Well,' said George, '*I* think the effect of his isolation, and his mask, and the way he bosses the others about are all intended to make him seem different – sort of special and magic.'

'I'd love to see his face,' said Anne.

She didn't know it at the time, but her curiosity was soon to be satisfied. The children had been living among the Jivaros for three days now, and it seemed like longer. They went for a walk in the village on the evening of the third day, and they were just passing the witch doctor's hut when the two Indian women who looked after him came out, chattering away to each other. Then Rna himself appeared in the doorway. He made signs to the children, telling them to come in.

'I wonder what he wants?' said George to herself, rather worried.

She didn't even realise that she'd spoken the words out loud, in an undertone, so she was very surprised to hear an unknown voice behind her say, 'Nothing alarming, young people, so set your minds at rest!'

George and her cousins swung round. Who had

said that? There wasn't anyone in the hut except for themselves and the mysterious Rna.

Then, to their enormous surprise, they saw the witch doctor take off the terrifying mask that hid his face – and his face itself came into view! The four children all exclaimed in chorus.

'A European!' cried Julian.

'And you speak English!' said Dick.

'But – who *are* you?' asked George.

Anne just squeaked in amazement and then stared at Rna with her mouth open!

The 'witch doctor' stepped forward and smiled at the children. He was about thirty-five, with hair as fair as Julian's and Anne's, blue eyes with little wrinkles under them, and a rather pale face. There was a frank, honest look in his intelligent eyes, but his mouth had a bitter twist to it.

'I see I've given you a surprise!' he said. He certainly had – the children were still stunned by this revelation! 'As you can guess, Rna is only a kind of part I have to play. Let me introduce myself: my real name is Guy Latham, and I'm an aviator – in fact I used to be quite a well-known aviator before I became a Jivaro witch doctor instead!'

'Oh, *I* know who you are!' cried Julian. 'The newspapers were all full of you a couple of years ago! I remember reading lots of things about your daring adventures. You were *very* well-known

until —'

'Until my last flight over the Brazilian forests put an end to all that!' said the airman, with a melancholy sigh.

'But what happened to you?' asked George.

'I had engine trouble, and I tried to land but my plane went out of control — it was a pure miracle I got out of it alive. I could see my best hope was to parachute out, and I came down right here, just in front of the chief's hut! I thought I'd be killed on the spot, or at least taken prisoner, but not a bit of it. The Jivaros aren't a bad lot at bottom. They're poorly organised, that's their trouble, and their chief hasn't got much of a grip on things. Anyway, when they saw a fair, blue-eyed man falling from the sky they thought I was one of their gods. I was supposed to be Kaloum-Kaloum, the god of the winds!'

George ventured to interrupt. 'Surely even the Jivaros know what a plane is — and that its pilot is only human?'

'A plane, yes! They see aircraft passing overhead from time to time. But a parachute is another matter! And you have to remember this tribe is one of the few remaining with almost no contact with the civilised world.'

Guy Latham paused for a moment, and then sighed, and went on.

'I suppose I was lucky, really. The plane itself

came down quite a way off, and the Jivaros didn't see it or hear it. The wind had carried me along like a leaf in the direction of their village. And when they saw me touch down, as if I'd come from the sky, they thought I must be their god, Kaloum-Kaloum.'

'Didn't you put them right about that?' asked Dick.

'Well, partly! I told them I wasn't Kaloum-Kaloum himself, but a messenger of his.'

'How did you manage to talk to them?' asked Dick.

'They knew a few words of Portuguese, and luckily I could already speak a few words of their dialect. That was just enough – and anyway, the less a messenger from the sky talks the more mysterious and impressive he seems! I can speak fluent Jivaro now. The chief and all the villagers look up to me – they think I bring them luck, and I can do what I like, just as long as I don't leave the village.'

'Why not?' asked Anne.

'Well, you see their point of view! I turned up at a moment when there was a bad shortage of game, and there'd been a drought, which made things even worse for the Indians, poor creatures. As chance would have it, the very day I arrived the hunters of the tribe killed several wild pigs in the forest, and the rain began to fall. So after that the Jivaros didn't want to let me go! I was too precious to be allowed to leave. And now I've taken you under my protection and painted you in Kaloum-Kaloum's own colours you're as sacred as I am, or nearly!'

The Five were thinking that this explained the witch doctor's strange behaviour, dressing them up in odd clothes and painting their faces.

'The Jivaros keep close watch on me, for fear of losing me,' the airman went on. 'The mask I wear is the symbol of my magic powers – and a very inconvenient symbol too, but I've had to get used to it! The chief believes that only he has the right to see my real face!'

'Haven't you ever thought of escaping?' asked George.

'Have I not! Time and time again! But what can one man do alone in the virgin forest, so far from civilisation? However, now you must tell me about yourselves! How did *you* get here? This is the first time I've had a real chance to talk to you on your own. My servants don't often leave the hut, and it would seem odd of the powerful Rna to go and visit children.'

George, as spokesman for the Five, told the airman all about their adventures with the hijackers.

'And if Luke, Marco and Josh do get back to civilisation, they'll send help and we'll *all* be rescued!' she finished.

'*If* they get back – and then *if* they bother about us any more, and *if* the Jivaros don't murder us first!' muttered Dick, between his teeth.

'Cheerful company, aren't you?' remarked Julian ironically.

There was silence. Guy Latham seemed to be deep in gloomy thoughts of his own. Julian was looking daggers at his brother – really, it was too bad of Dick to make things worse when they were in such trouble already! Dick himself was sulking. George was thinking hard and Timmy, gazing devotedly at her, seemed to be worried. He was very sensitive to her feelings, and he knew instinctively that all was not well with his mistress.

'If only I could have salvaged the radio equipment from my plane!' sighed Guy Latham. 'Then we could have sent out an SOS!'

It was Anne who cried, unexpectedly, 'Oh, but there *is* a radio on board the plane *we* came in!'

Chapter Seven

A LEGEND OF TREASURE

'At least, there *was* a radio,' Anne added. 'But the transmitter's only half mended, and –'

The 'witch doctor' started, and seemed to come to life. '*What* did you say, my dear? Radio equipment? Do you mean it?'

Julian knew more about the technical side of the radio problem than the others – he had watched Marco at work trying to repair it, and lent a hand now and then. He told Guy Latham as much as he could. Frowning, the airman thought it over.

'Listen,' he said at last. 'Somehow or other, I've got to get to that crashed plane and see if it's at all possible to repair the transmitter.'

'But the plane's an awfully long way off,' George pointed out.

'It's not as far as you think, in fact,' the airman told her. 'I can place it pretty well from your description of the spot where you crashed. That hill overlooking the Yapura is a landmark, and a good point of reference. You must have gone a long way round to get here. I know a short cut which would get me there in about an hour.'

'I thought you said you weren't allowed to leave the village?' asked Julian.

'Well, in a manner of speaking I'm not—it would be more like it to say I can't leave the Jivaros. But I've often been with them when they go out hunting in the forest, so I know these parts quite well.'

'But,' objected Dick, 'once you've seen the plane how will you manage to get back there on your own and work on repairing the radio transmitter? The Jivaros will never let you do *that*!'

Guy Latham smiled at the children. 'Up till now I never really tried to escape,' he said. 'I knew I was sure to die on my own in the forest. But I can slip away easily enough if I want to, for a few hours.'

That night George, Julian, Dick and Anne slept better than they had for some time. And next morning, when the Indian woman came to bring them their breakfast of fruit and manioc cakes, as usual, they found a little note from Guy hidden underneath a papaya.

'Couldn't resist the temptation to go and find that plane last night,' he had written. 'All's well!

Marco had a part fitted the wrong way round! I put that right, and the radio's back in working order. I've sent out one SOS already. No luck so far, but I'll try again whenever I get the chance.'

Dick and George were so thrilled by this news that they went out of the hut to dance a jig! Timmy joined in too, barking as he jumped and bounded around them. Julian and Anne watched, laughing. Some of the Jivaro children, hearing all this merriment, came running up and started dancing too. What a noise they all made! Then Tofi, the chief's son, arrived. He was a boy of about sixteen, with a manner that was gentle as well as proud. The Five liked him a great deal. He began laughing and dancing about too.

The chief himself, hearing all this racket, came striding up, but when he saw his son having such a good time he smiled and went away again, nodding his head. George dug Dick in the ribs.

'To think we were scared of the savage Jivaros! Why, they're as gentle as lambs when you get to know them!'

'I'll be glad to get away from them, all the same,' said Dick. 'Let's hope Guy's SOS gets through to someone.'

Now that they had some hope of rescue, the children found it easier to take things as they came. Guy Latham managed to have a private word with them almost every evening. He went back to the plane whenever he got a chance, but so far the SOS messages he broadcast didn't seem to have been heard by anyone.

The four cousins did their best to pass the time while they waited. They were firm friends with Tofi now. They were even beginning to learn a little of the Jivaro language – and they could always make signs too. Soon they and Tofi could have quite long conversations, and it was during one of these conversations that they heard a story which fascinated them, because it was so mysterious.

The fact was, the Five liked *anything* mysterious! They had solved a lot of difficult problems already, and felt that they were almost experts in the mystery line! 'Remember how we prevented that burglary at Manners House?' George said to her cousins. 'And unmasked the spies in Scotland, and got Sir Donald Riddington's valuable collection of gold watches back for him, and found our friend Tinker's pet cheetah? Why shouldn't we solve *this* mystery, too?'

'Because for one thing, we're not in the British Isles; we're in the middle of the South American jungle, and for another, it's a very, very tricky one!' Dick told her, smiling. 'Personally I can't even make out just what Tofi's telling us. He keeps on repeating the same words, something about treasure, and temple, and moon, and forest.'

Tofi nodded hard as he recognised these words, and repeated, 'Yes, yes – treasure! Temple! Forest!'

'Oh, bother!' said Dick. 'We won't get any further *this* way! I tell you what, let's ask Guy if *he* knows the story about the treasure when we see him this evening!'

And so they did. When he heard what was interesting the children so much, Guy smiled.

'It's an old Jivaro legend,' he told them. 'And like all legends, I suppose it has a grain of truth in it. The difficult part is deciding what's true and what's invented! Nobody knows exactly what the treasure itself *is*, but it's supposed to be buried in the heart of the forest in the Temple of the Moon, a ruin left by a civilised people who were rather like the Incas. Their civilisation has died out now, of course.'

'I say, how fascinating!' said George.

'Woof!' agreed Timmy, looking interested.

'So you want to know more, Tim? All right!' said Guy, laughing. 'The legend is a very old one, but the Jivaros are naturally rather lazy, and they don't think it's important enough for them to set off on an expedition to look for the treasure. The way their minds work, "treasure" doesn't sound very interesting if it means gold or precious stones, as the legend suggests. Their own idea of a treasure is plenty of game, a good manioc harvest and other such gifts of Nature.'

'Yes, I see,' said George. 'If we wanted them to help look for this treasure we'd have to think of some reason that really interested them, and stimulated them to take action!'

'That's right,' Guy Latham told her. 'And as a matter of fact, now's your moment! The Jivaros would be inclined to like the idea because . . .' And he stopped, just teasing them, and looked at them with a twinkle in his eye.

'Oh, go *on!*' said Dick impatiently. 'Because *what?*'

'Because according to this legend of theirs, the treasure can only be found *by children!*' the aviator-cum-witch-doctor explained.

'I say! This is great!' cried George, jumping up. She was full of excitement. 'So we've got a really good chance! We'd better strike while the iron is hot – oh, Guy, couldn't you persuade the chief to organise an expedition? Tell him the treasure we want to find is a really marvellous good-luck charm, better than having all of *us* in the village! Oh *yes!* That's it! The treasure will be our ransom, don't you see? It will pay him for setting us free!'

'Now, now – calm down!' Guy told her. 'You haven't found this treasure yet, and there's very little chance of finding it even with Jivaro help. All we know is that it's supposed to be "in the heart of the forest" – and those directions aren't very much to go by!'

'Are you *sure* the legend doesn't say anything more definite?'

'Well, it says something more, even if it's not very definite,' Guy admitted. 'Yes, there *are* directions for finding the treasure – if you can solve the threefold riddle that gives you the clue! The riddle has been handed down orally from generation to generation, and of course that means it may have been wrongly passed on. I wouldn't expect much help from it.'

'We can always try, though,' George insisted. 'I mean, if the treasure was *very* far from here it's not likely the Jivaros would have heard of it, is it? Come on, Guy! Won't you ask Pfo to let us try our luck?'

The airman smiled. 'Well, why not?' he said. 'But I don't know that I'll get anywhere with him – and I don't know that he'd take kindly to the idea of swapping some imaginary treasure for our freedom.'

'But once we've found the treasure it won't *be* imaginary any more,' Dick pointed out, very confidently.

Guy shook his head. 'It's all a bit childish, really – still, I can always try! Fortune favours the brave, don't they say?'

And so next day Rna the 'witch doctor' went to see Pfo, the chief, and they had a long consultation in Pfo's big hut. George and her cousins sat outside the chief's hut, waiting. When Rna came out, the hideous mask hiding his face meant that the children couldn't guess how the interview had gone. But Rna signed to them to go into Pfo's hut themselves. He followed them in. The chief was squatting on a mat, and Tofi was with his father. He looked at his new friends with eyes that sparkled with interest.

Pfo rose, walked round the group of children, touched them respectfully with one finger, and nodded his head several times. Tofi too went over to Julian, George, Dick and Anne, smiled at them and shook hands in the way they had taught him. His handshake seemed to express admiration, confidence and hope all at once.

'Seems to be going all right,' muttered George, in an undertone.

Guy Latham smiled behind his mask. Yes, it *was* going all right! Pfo had allowed his witch doctor to win him over, as Guy told the Five later when they all met in his hut.

Timmy, sitting on his haunches, seemed to be listening as eagerly as the children themselves.

'I brought Pfo round to the idea,' Guy said. 'I told him that as you were messengers from heaven, sent by Kaloum-Kaloum just as I was, you were the ones who could find the treasure of the legend. Pfo wasn't too enthusiastic at first – as I told you,

89

the idea of "treasure" doesn't mean anything much to him. But I went on, and I kept saying I'd heard the voice of Kaloum-Kaloum last night!'

George laughed. 'Come to that, so did I!' she said. 'He's the god of the wind isn't he? And there was a *strong* wind last night!'

'That's right,' Guy agreed. 'I told the chief that Kaloum-Kaloum had breathed his message in my ear. And I said the treasure in the legend was a powerful amulet which would bring the Jivaros great good luck once they had it: good hunting, rich harvests, long years of health and a victory over their enemies.'

'I say, we're worth a lot, aren't we?' Dick remarked. 'Now I see why Tofi shook hands so enthusiastically!'

'Yes, that's the point – *are* we worth it?' asked Julian. 'Did Pfo say we could go and look for the treasure, and if so, would he swap it for our freedom?'

'The answer to all that is yes!' Guy told the boy. 'He's going to organise an expedition straight away, so let's hope for the best! It will be wonderful if you *do* succeed. Because then the Jivaros will let you go – they'll even help you! And you can be sure I'll manage to leave with you, somehow or other.'

Pfo was a careful, slow-moving sort of character who obviously never acted on impulse, but when he did decide on something he put his whole heart into it. Rna said the young messengers who came from Kaloum-Kaloum were to go and look for the treasure of the legend, and that was good enough for him! He, Pfo, would be one of their escort himself, along with his best warriors and his most faithful servants. They would take weapons and provisions. Everything had been thought of!

As for Tofi, the chief's son, he was bubbling over with enthusiasm. He was simply delighted that he could go on the expedition too. He followed the Five wherever they went, like a faithful dog.

'Like dear old Tim, in fact!' said George, smiling.

But Julian was in a rather more serious mood. Like Guy, he saw the other side of things, and knew how important this expedition was.

'It's all very well if we do find the treasure,' he told the others, 'but if we fail, we'll be in a more difficult position than we are now – and so will Guy! The Jivaros will bear us a grudge for rousing their hopes and then disappointing them – who knows, they might take revenge?'

'Oh, Julian, do you really think so?' asked Anne anxiously.

'Don't worry!' said George, full of confidence. 'You *know* the Five never fail to solve a mystery!'

'Well, for a start let's try solving this riddle,' said Julian. 'What exactly does it say again? Let's have a look, Dick – hand it over, will you?'

Chapter Eight

RIDDLES – AND DANGERS!

Guy Latham had told the children how the three parts of the riddle went, and Dick had carefully copied it all down in the little notebook he always carried with him. The children already knew the riddle by heart, but they thought they might suddenly get a bright idea if they looked at the words on paper again.

They went over to sit under a huge tree at the edge of the clearing, and studied the riddle. Tofi and Timmy both watched the four cousins hopefully, as if they felt sure they'd soon solve it!

Guy Latham, watching from a distance, wasn't so sure. He was feeling rather angry with himself. Now that the expedition was all settled, he was afraid they might have been too rash.

'I ought at least to have waited to see if George and the others *could* solve the riddle,' he told himself, 'and then discussed the expedition with Pfo. But George was so keen I let her have her way, and now we're committed to looking for the treasure and we can't turn back. Pfo is taking it very seriously.'

He was all the more worried because he'd tried solving the riddle himself in the past, just for something to do, and got nowhere with it!

Meanwhile George was lying flat on her front on the mossy ground, studying the words in front of her.

'The sun will fall in the middle of the pool,' she read out loud. 'Then you will see the setting moon in the west. The yellow goddess beyond will look at you, green-eyed.'

'Three separate riddles, but all linked together,' said Julian slowly. 'I hope they're in the right order, and haven't got mixed up over the years!'

'I should think they are,' said Anne. 'I mean, the second sentence begins "then" as if it *ought* to follow on from the first, and the third one, with that "beyond", sounds as if it should come last.'

'I think Anne's right,' said George.

'It's the "pool" that sounds easy, but *I* think is the difficult bit,' said Dick. 'It's so vague! And how can the sun actually fall into a pool, that's what I'd like to know!'

'Surely it must mean the sun *sets*,' said Anne.

'No, it doesn't,' Julian told her. 'I specially

asked Guy about that, and he says the Jivaros use quite a different word for the sun setting. This definitely means the sun *falls* into the water.'

George was thinking hard, and frowning with the effort.

'Maybe it doesn't mean the sun itself falls into the pool,' she suggested. 'Maybe it means the *reflection* of the sun. And when it says the *middle* of the pool, it's telling us we have to look at a certain time of day . . .'

'At mid-day!' Julian suddenly shouted, triumphantly. 'Wouldn't the sun be reflected in the very middle of a pool of water at mid-day? Gosh – George, I think that's it! We must find this pool, and wait until mid-day for – for I'm not at all sure what! Who's got that riddle? How exactly does the next bit go?'

'Then you will see the setting moon in the west,' George read out.

Julian's face fell. 'That's not much good, is it? I mean, it simply doesn't make sense. Suppose we do find the right pool, we're not going to see the moon setting while the sun's at its height! In fact we're not going to see the moon setting in the west anyway, not with all those forest trees growing so tall and getting in the way!'

'No, I don't get that part of the riddle either, Ju,' his cousin admitted. 'However, the first part does give us something to start with! Remember Guy telling us about the great stretch of marshes some miles away from here? They must be full of pools. I bet it's one of them — a pool in the marshes that could reflect the sun at mid-day!'

'But Guy said it was hard-going to get to the marshes,' Julian reminded her. 'We'd have to make our way through some very thick vegetation, and go extremely slowly.'

'Who cares how slowly we go, so long as we get there in the end?' said George, completely dismissing her cautious cousin's objection. 'Now then, what about the third part of the riddle?'

Tofi leaned over to look at the sheet of paper, even though the mysterious black marks on it meant nothing at all to him.

'The yellow goddess beyond will look at you, green-eyed . . . Well, *that's* simple enough!' said George confidently.

'Is it?' said Anne. *She* didn't think it was in the least simple!

'Yes, of course! Think, Anne, think!'

Anne frowned, and then smiled. 'Oh, I see now!' she said. 'The third bit means the treasure itself! 'The "yellow goddess" must be an idol!'

'I worked that out for myself, too,' agreed Dick. 'A yellow idol — gosh, it's probably made of solid gold!'

'With green eyes,' George reminded him. 'Precious stones, I bet!'

'Possibly emeralds,' said Julian, getting quite excited! 'In fact, *probably* emeralds. They mine wonderful emeralds in Brazil – and it was quite usual to make idols out of precious metals and jewels in the time of the ancient civilisations!'

Dick couldn't sit still any longer! He just had to get up and start dancing for joy. 'We'll do it! We'll do it!' he chanted.

Watching the children, Guy saw how cheerful they were, and realised they must be on their way to solving the riddle. That made him feel a little better.

Meanwhile Pfo himself was making preparations for the expedition to find the distant and mysterious temple of the moon. The marshes began some miles away from the Jivaro village, and they stretched a long way. And when the expedition did set off they made slow progress, just as Julian had foreseen. Some of the Jivaro warriors and hunters went ahead as scouts. They were followed by Pfo and his son Tofi, Guy – or rather, Rna the witch doctor! – and the Five. Several porters brought up the rear of the procession.

The day before they set off, Guy had gone back to the wrecked plane to broadcast another SOS. As usual, he got no reply.

'Too bad!' he had said to the children. 'Well, we mustn't be down-hearted! I'll go on putting out my calls when we get back.'

Now, however, he was thinking, '*If* we get back.' The scouts had a lot of hard work cutting back creepers with their machetes. The children found they were sweating profusely. Poor old Timmy was panting and looking very unhappy. His tongue was hanging out the whole time. Suddenly George saw the dog stop. Raising his muzzle, he began to growl deep inside his throat.

The Jivaros had stopped all of a sudden, too. Like the dog, they had picked up a dangerous scent!

'It's a jaguar!' Guy whispered to the children.

Julian, Dick, George and Anne shivered. They knew the jaguar was the fiercest animal in the Brazilian jungle. An adult jaguar weighs about a hundred and fifty kilograms and has great stamina. Its speed and suppleness are really remarkable. The one whose scent Tim and the Indians had picked up couldn't be far away . . .

Pfo picked up his rifle – it was a very good one, and Guy had often wondered where he got it and all the ammunition he seemed to have for it. Signing to the others not to move, he slipped soundlessly into the undergrowth. They heard just one shot – and then silence!

George, holding Tim's collar in one hand and keeping his mouth closed with the other, couldn't help jumping.

But Pfo reappeared almost at once, smiling. The

Jivaros knew what that meant. They rushed forward with shouts of triumph, and soon came back dragging their chief's victim. It was a really enormous jaguar! Beaming, they all praised the chief, and then they went on again. The Five were feeling a good deal more scared about the whole expedition now than they had when it was first planned!

It took them the better part of two days to reach the marshes, and George and her cousins were very glad when they got there at last. They hadn't much enjoyed their slow progress through the forest, or spending the night by a smoky camp fire among all the sounds of the Brazilian jungle. They felt it was full of dangers that might leap out and attack.

Julian, George, Dick and Anne hadn't known quite what to expect the marshes would be like. The forest didn't actually come to an end, but there were long channels of water that appeared among the huge tree trunks, winding their way past them, dark and deep and foul-smelling, until they came out in great stretches of water which were more or less stagnant.

The expedition was going along a muddy bank when Dick suddenly let out a cry. He had just been going to step on what looked like a log when it moved and dived into the water.

'An alligator!' Guy told him. 'They're dangerous

– careful where you put your feet!'

Up till now Guy had been careful not to talk too much to the children in front of the Jivaros. He didn't want to give the impression that they were all in league. But this journey had brought them all closer together and Guy thought that, all things considered, messengers of the god Kaloum-Kaloum might be expected to talk to each other in the god's own language – which of course was English! As for the Jivaros themselves, they weren't keeping much of a watch on their witch doctor and the children. Pfo knew quite well that there wasn't any real way they could give him the slip, unless they flew right up into the sky again.

The little party had a long march that day. The banks of the channels were made of a kind of spongy black soil, and gave way easily underfoot. The Jivaros and their friends had wrapped banana leaves round their legs and feet and tied them in place with creepers. These primitive boots kept off the worst of the stinking mud and the insect bites.

Anne was feeling tired, and a little bit feverish too.

'How are we ever going to find the particular pool the riddle is talking about?' she wailed quietly in the evening. 'It's like looking for a needle in a haystack!'

'We've already passed quite a lot of pools and lakes,' Julian reminded her.

'Yes, and there was nothing to show that they were the place we're after! Anyway, the water was so dark and murky, and the trees grew so close over it, the sun could hardly "fall into the middle".'

'All the same,' said Dick, frowning thoughtfully, 'one of those pools could be the right one after all. The legend is so old that the trees have had time to grow where they may not have grown before!'

Guy shook his head. 'I see what you mean, Dick, but I think the riddle must refer to a really big pool or even a lake somewhere. It was probably the last of the priests of the Temple of the Moon who thought the three riddles up, at a time when they saw their civilisation going downhill. They'll have worked out that a small pool might disappear, or trees might grow up round it. So the points of reference they left will have been something solid – chosen especially because they *would* last through the centuries!'

'Well, let's hope so!' said George.

Next day they came to a tributary of the Yapura which flowed right into the forest. Seeing that the children were worn out, Guy had a consultation with the chief. Pfo himself was upset to see how tired all the young people were, including his son Tofi, and he decided that they would stop for a whole day's rest.

The children appreciated the chance to stop for a day. The expedition's stocks of provisions had gone down a good deal, so the hunters and Pfo set off into the trees to look for game. Meanwhile, Guy, Tofi and the Five strolled along a beach of white sand beside the little river. Its waters were very clear. Guy felt he couldn't bear to wear the heavy witch doctor mask any more, so he took it off and suggested a bathe. Tofi seemed to feel he was greatly honoured by being allowed to see the witch doctor's face.

Of course Guy made sure there were no alligators about before they went into the water for their dip. He kept watch while Julian, Dick, George, Anne and Tofi bathed. Then Guy had a bathe himself. Timmy was having a wonderful time splashing about in the water.

'Tofi!' called George. 'Throw Timmy a branch – look, like this! You wait – he'll bring it back to you!'

Timmy started swimming towards the floating branch. Tofi was delighted to see the dog take it in his mouth and start back to the bank when George called him. But suddenly the young Jivaro's smile froze on his lips. His complexion changed colour to a sort of grey-green! George followed the direction of his eyes – and a shiver of horror ran through her.

There was a truly enormous snake on the opposite bank of the river. It was just uncoiling itself and getting ready to swim across!

Guy had seen the huge snake too. 'An anaconda!' he whispered, stunned by the sight. 'The biggest snake in the world – and one of the toughest to tackle!'

Tofi's teeth were chattering. '*Canoudi – canoudi!*' he kept stammering. That was obviously the Jivaro word for an anaconda.

Timmy started barking as hard as he could. George was the first to pull herself together.

'Quick – we've got to do something!' she gasped.

The anaconda looked as if it was five to six metres long. And its body was so thick that it looked even longer. George's shout had shaken Guy into action. 'Quick! Copy me!' he shouted. 'Take some of the creepers the porters were carrying and beat the water with them as hard as you can – maybe we can scare it off like that!'

Doing their best to overcome their fear, the children did as he said. They whipped the water up with the creepers as hard as they could.

'But Guy – snakes are deaf, aren't they?' shouted Dick. 'It won't even hear us, surely?'

'No – but it can see us, and feel the water moving,' Guy shouted back. He was still frantically whipping up the surface of the water. 'It won't want to get into the whirlpool we're making.'

And he was right. The strange movement of the water and the sight of these odd, upright, two-legged figures capering about upset the snake – and so did the sight of the other creature, the one with four legs, which wasn't a bit like a monkey or

any other animal it knew. All things considered, the huge snake decided it would be more sensible to turn back. Deciding not to attack, nor just to go back to the bank it had left, it slipped into the current of the river, which carried it away. The last the children saw of it was its great, long body, with black spots on an olive-green background, swimming away downstream.

'Phew!' said George. '*That* was a narrow escape!'

Chapter Nine

THE RIDDLE IS SOLVED

The children and Tofi were very grateful to Guy, whose clever notion had saved them from the snake.

'I wouldn't have fancied ending up inside that monster!' said Dick. 'I'd even rather it ended up inside me!'

Guy laughed. 'Well, you might do worse, you know. All snakes are edible, and the big ones like our friend there taste particularly good! Would you like to try snake some time?'

'Oh, *no!*' cried the children, in chorus.

'Thank you all the same,' Anne added politely.

'All right, all right!' laughed Guy. 'I won't make you. But – '

He was interrupted by Pfo and his companions, coming back from their hunt. The Jivaros seemed worried, and were unusually quiet. They had no game with them at all. Pfo hurried up to his witch doctor, who had hastily put the mask back on, and told him something in a low voice, with a great many gestures.

In a moment Guy translated for the children, speaking in an undertone. 'Apparently they found tracks which suggest their enemies the Trakos are somewhere nearby. The Trakos are fierce warriors, always fighting other tribes. So don't make any noise. The idea is that we'll stay here without moving and wait for the Trakos to go away. It looks as if they're on the trail of a jaguar.'

But unfortunately it didn't look as if the Trakos *were* going to go away. One of their scouts had spotted Pfo and followed him. The children could already hear furtive little sounds of people moving in the undergrowth. Timmy's hair stood on end all along his spine.

'Ssh, Timmy!' breathed George. 'Keep quiet, good old Timmy!'

Pfo signalled to his men to keep quiet too. The hunters grasped their old guns – Pfo himself was the only one who had a good, modern rifle – and the porters held their spears and bows at the ready. They were all on the alert.

'I expect the Trakos think we've shot some big game,' said Guy in a low voice. 'And they're planning to get it away from us. We *haven't* caught any game, but they'll take what provisions we do have if they get a chance!'

George was feeling very indignant. It was awful to think of letting the Trakos get away with their provisions and equipment! In fact she was so angry that she quite forgot to be frightened. After all they'd gone through, *she* didn't intend to be left here in the middle of the forest – close to the treasure they were looking for, maybe, but unable to go either on or back for lack of food and all the rest of their gear!

As for Dick, he was feeling very alarmed indeed. He could tell, from the expression on Tofi's face, that the Trako Indians must be formidable enemies.

George looked at her cousin Anne. Anne was being very brave indeed – she wasn't trembling, though she had gone very pale, and she was holding Julian's hand tight.

'Oh, I do *hope* the Trakos won't do anything to hurt poor Anne!' thought George. It wasn't her own danger she minded – but she was very worried about her gentle little cousin. 'I don't think I could bear that. You couldn't either, could you, Timmy dear?'

She saw her dog's brave, trusting eyes raised to her. And the sight suddenly galvanised her into action! All at once George thought of a clever trick!

'Quick, Guy!' she whispered. 'Let me have your mask! And that bunch of plumes the porters put on

108

top of their load!'

Guy couldn't think why she wanted those things, but he did as the clever girl said. It was the work of a moment for George to fasten the ornamental bunch of plumes to Timmy's back. She herself put on the enormous mask. It had plumes on top of it, too, so that the whole thing entirely hid her head and covered her shoulders.

Then she ran forward, followed by Timmy. Stunned by the sight of this strange apparition, Pfo let her pass without doing anything to stop her. He was too surprised to react at all!

At that very moment the curtain of greenery separating the forest from the riverside beach parted suddenly, and a dozen athletic-looking Trako Indians rushed out to tackle the Jivaros. But they didn't get far! At the sight of George and her dog, in their weird feathered outfits, the leader of the Trakos stopped short. The war-cry he had been about to utter died away in his throat. George and Timmy really did look very, very surprising.

The mask George was wearing weighed very heavily – she felt as if it were crushing her, and she could hardly breathe. All the same, she kept on waving her arms and leaping about, letting out a whole series of simply blood-curdling yells. The mask itself acted as a kind of amplifier, making them sound even worse, and they encouraged Timmy to bark too. George and Timmy – what a

duet! It went in time to George's wild skipping about.

The Jivaros were just as scared as their enemies! They couldn't take their eyes off the small but monstrous figure leaping about in front of them, making the most terrible groaning sounds. Then, suddenly, George went into the attack. She pointed straight at the leader of the Trako warriors and shouted, 'Get him, Timmy – go on, *bite him*!'

Timmy was more than ready to do as she said. He bounded forward and sank his teeth right into – the place where the bold Trako leader's calf *had* been a moment before! But the bold Trako leader hadn't waited for him. He had turned tail and fled, along with his equally bold warriors!

The Jivaros had won the victory, and without shedding a drop of blood either. Pfo and his hunters began jumping for joy, and the porters waved their spears and bows in the air to show how happy they were. Tofi clapped his hands.

Now came the moment when George had to hand back the witch doctor's mask. She turned solemnly to Guy. He showed he could act a part just as well as she could! With great ceremony, he took it off her and slowly put it back on his own head. It was as if he were taking back his magic powers after lending them to George so that she could defeat the Trakos.

When the rejoicings had died down a bit, the

Jivaros turned to the little girl who had saved them. Pfo solemnly took off his own necklace of jaguar's teeth and put it round George's neck. Then he knelt down in front of her and put a part of her red and yellow waistcoat to his forehead.

George felt dreadfully embarrassed. It was obviously an act of homage, and she didn't know how to react. The best she could think of was to lay her hand on the chief's head. Everyone shouted joyfully, and George realised that, very luckily, she had instinctively guessed the right thing to do.

Once they were all rather calmer, Julian, Dick and Anne patted Timmy, and hugged and congratulated George. Then the four of them wondered what to do next. The most sensible thing seemed to be to set out again, but give the Trakos' hunting grounds as wide a berth as possible, and in fact that was just what Pfo and Guy thought too.

'The only trouble is that we may pass the pool we want without ever actually seeing it,' said Julian.

'Yes,' agreed Anne, 'but after what's just happened I'm inclined to believe in our luck! The new route we're going to take may bring us *closer* to the pool of the riddle instead of farther away from it.'

'Yes, we've got to trust to luck!' Dick agreed.

'I just hope we don't have any *more* encounters with jaguars or snakes or fierce Indians in the forest!' said George. Even she had had enough excitement for a little while.

They didn't meet with any more actual dangers, but there were other difficulties along their way. There was very little game to be caught, and food had to be rationed out. And as they moved farther from the Yapura they had to go carefully with water, too. It was getting more and more difficult to move through the thick undergrowth of the forest at all. The Five began to feel exhausted. Poor Timmy was covered in ticks, and the children were being attacked by them as well.

Next evening, Tofi told his father that he couldn't go any farther unless he had a good night's rest. Pfo agreed to stop, and he had fires lit and posted guards. The whole camp went to sleep. It was not a very long night, but at least it was a restful one, and they set off feeling refreshed next morning at dawn.

As the sun rose higher, it got hotter and hotter, and soon everyone was feeling terribly thirsty. However the witch doctor assured Pfo that they would soon find water. Guy was taking a big chance – he was only guessing, and he thought that if his prediction turned out wrong, the Indians might well stop believing in his magic powers! Indeed, they might turn against him . . .

But he needn't have worried. Sure enough, they actually did come within sight of a great stretch of clear water at about noon. The Jivaros ran down to the lake, flung themselves on all fours and drank greedily. Guy scooped up some water in the tortoise shell which he used as a cup, and took the precaution of dissolving a little brown tablet in it.

'That will make it safe to drink,' he told the children. 'Luckily I had a good stock of these tablets on me when I had to parachute out of my plane. I go slow with them, of course. But I don't think we can wait to boil water just now.'

The children quenched their thirst with great enjoyment, while Timmy joined the Jivaros drinking straight from the lake. When they had all finished drinking, the sun was at its highest point in the sky – and suddenly Anne let out a cry.

'Look, look! The sun – it's reflected in the very middle of the lake. This is the water the riddle was talking about!'

'Hang on – we can't be sure!' said George. 'It might be reflected in another lake or pool as well.'

'The sun will fall in the middle of the pool,' Julian remembered, quoting the proverb, 'and then you will see the setting moon in the west.'

'Well, no setting moon in sight, obviously!' said Dick, sounding disappointed.

Guy took a compass out of his pocket and looked at it. The Jivaros watched him with great interest.

'West is over there,' he said, pointing to part of the forest where the undergrowth looked particularly thick. 'Even if the moon did happen to be just on the horizon at this moment, we couldn't possibly see it!'

'Just as I thought all along,' said Julian gloomily.

'Wait a minute!' cried George. 'Look – oh, do look!'

She was pointing to something in the west, the same way as Guy had pointed, over by the trees. And then everyone, including the Jivaros, let out a cry of amazement. They saw a stone disk almost four metres tall standing not far from the pool. It was a perfect circle. But the most striking thing about it was the luminous light, silvery, almost pearly, which it was giving off in full daylight. It really did look almost as if the moon itself had come down to earth to stand there on a sort of platform made of reddish rock.

Guy and the children couldn't understand this strange phenomenon at first. Then they realised what caused it. The rays of the sun, reflected off the water, were shining on a whole series of little mirrors set into the disk at different angles. The stone itself gave a silvery look to the reflected light and made this strange opalescent effect.

'Why, it's just a trick!' marvelled George. 'All done with mirrors!'

'A very clever trick, though, you must admit,' said Dick. 'And now we've found what we are looking for, that's the main thing.'

'It explains the second part of the riddle, too,' added Anne. 'So now all we have to do is find the idol!'

The light was already fading in intensity. As the sun sank from its highest point, the disk didn't shine so brightly, and in the end it looked just like a perfectly ordinary round stone blending in with its surroundings.

Guy turned back to the Jivaros, and made them a little speech. They all shouted with joy. He had as much power over the Indians as ever – his predictions had come true. The water had appeared, and it looked as if the English children were about to discover the treasure! George went over to the stone 'moon', followed by her cousins and by Timmy.

'The yellow goddess beyond,' she was muttering, 'will look at you, green-eyed.'

The forest here seemed thicker than ever, but the Jivaros set to work to hack out a path with new vigour. They attacked the lush undergrowth with their machetes, and the little procession went on for about three hundred metres. And suddenly, Guy and the children knew for sure that they had found the fabulous Temple of the Moon at last!

It couldn't be anything else! An extraordinary building lay ahead of them. It was white, and the front of it was a most unusual shape: the shape of a crescent moon. A huge circular doorway stood right in the middle of it, and seemed to be inviting them in.

Obviously feeling overawed, the Jivaros hung back. They dared not go any further. George gave herself a little shake.

'Come on!' she said. 'The goddess with the green eyes must be waiting for us in there!'

'Yes, and it wouldn't be polite to keep her waiting any longer,' added Dick, laughing.

But much to the children's surprise, Guy suddenly gestured to them to keep quiet. 'Go carefully!' he whispered. 'Look at that!'

By 'that' he meant three back-packs, a very recent type and almost brand new, standing on the ground beside the entrance to the temple!

'My goodness – explorers, do you think?' stammered Dick, in astonishment.

'No idea,' whispered Guy. 'But we'd better be very cautious, just to be on the safe side. Let's make sure we –'

But he didn't finish his sentence. Letting out a brief 'Woof!' Timmy was galloping forward. He obviously intended to race in through the doorway and enter the Temple of the Moon. George was taken by surprise, and was only just in time to call him to heel.

'Whatever has come over old Timmy?' said Dick.

'He's not acting as if he scented danger, is he?' said Guy, puzzled.

'No, not at all,' said George. 'He's acting more as if he scented somebody he knows!'

'But that's impossible,' said Julian. 'We don't know any explorers, except for Guy here, and –'

'Never mind that for now,' Guy interrupted him. 'I think I'll go on and scout ahead.'

However, the children weren't going to let Guy go into the temple alone. He realised that they meant it! So he gave in, and turned to Pfo, telling him to be ready to come to their aid if they needed him. Then he made his way cautiously from tree to tree and reached the temple entrance. The children followed him.

'All right, you've reached the temple – now just stay where you are!' he told them in a soft voice. He took his mask off, slipped through the circular opening, and disappeared.

George hesitated, but then she whispered, 'I'm going too. We can't possibly let him venture in there alone!'

'We'll all go,' Julian decided.

So the Five too entered the temple. It was very dim inside, and George almost collided with Guy, who had stopped to get his eyes used to the dark before he went on. He wasn't very pleased to find the Five had followed him after all, but they could hardly argue about it here and now!

It didn't take their eyes too long to get accustomed to the dim light filtering in through the openings in the temple walls. It was a vast building. Pillars of different heights stood in the shape of the crescent moon, and there was a flight of steps to the right and another to the left, leading up to the two horns of the crescent.

The left-hand horn ended on a kind of platform, where a great stone slab and a kind of throne stood.

'That must be the sacrificial stone,' whispered George. 'And the throne's for the priest or the witch doctor.'

'Ssh!' hissed Guy. He was very worried. He had just heard a sound from the right-hand horn, which was in the dark. But at that moment, a light suddenly went on over there, and a voice said, in English, 'There! Got this wretched torch working again at last!'

Chapter Ten

OLD ACQUAINTANCES

'Marco!' cried Dick. He knew that voice very well!

Someone swept the beam of a powerful electric torch round, and aimed it at Guy and the Five.

'Well, I never did!' exclaimed Marco. 'It's the kids – the kids and a stranger!'

Two more figures were already hurrying down the stairs to join Guy and the Five – Josh and Luke! Once they had recovered from their surprise, the children introduced everyone. Josh roared with laughter on hearing that Guy was also Rna, the Jivaro witch doctor. As for Luke, he smiled at Anne.

'I'm so glad to see you, Anne,' he said, sounding as if he meant it. 'Perhaps we'll manage to get back to civilisation between the lot of us.'

'You mean you haven't come back to rescue us?' said Julian, surprised.

'I'm afraid not,' Luke told him, sighing rather sadly. 'After we got away from the Jivaro village we went back to the plane to collect our back-packs and some canned food. And then . . . well, we got lost. We've been lost for quite a time, and we've only just found this extraordinary temple. And what's more, we've made an amazing discovery here – come and have a look!'

They all went up the steps to the horn of the crescent, where Marco was still standing with his torch. Guy and the children couldn't help exclaiming in admiration – for they found themselves facing an enormous solid gold idol. It was the figure of a woman wearing a crescent moon on her head, and with a veil of pure silver tissue round her golden shoulders. Her sparkling eyes were an amazing deep green.

'Emeralds!' said Marco proudly. 'We're going to take them out – we'll get a good price for them once we're back in Rio!'

And he moved towards the idol with a chisel in his hand. He was just going to insert it into the gold under the goddess's eyes – but Guy put out an arm to stop him.

'Just a minute!' he said drily. 'You haven't asked *us* how *we* come to be here ourselves. Well, here's our own story!'

And he told the three hijackers how he and the children had come here with the Jivaros specially to find the idol.

'Once Pfo has it,' he finished, 'he'll let us all go free, and then we can join the three of you and get back to civilisation together.'

Josh laughed in a very nasty way.

'But if you don't summon these Jivaros you're so friendly with,' he said, 'they'll never know we found the idol first, will they? And we can get out of here unseen – there's a little doorway round at the back of the temple opening straight into the jungle. Never mind the back-packs – they don't have much in them anyway. Go on, Marco, and hurry up about it!'

Marco picked his chisel up again, but Guy seized him by the wrist.

'Are you crazy?' he asked. 'Listen, this idol must be handed over to Pfo unharmed, or he'll never let the children go, or me either!'

'Who cares about you and the kids?' growled Josh. '*I* don't! Getting rich is what I care about!'

But now Luke took a hand. 'Josh, you'll never get rich if the Jivaros catch you and you can't escape from the jungle! Come on, can't you see sense? This is in all our interests!'

But obviously Marco and Josh *couldn't* see sense! The sight of the fabulous emeralds made them lose their heads entirely – they'd quite forgotten the danger they were in.

When Guy made another attempt to stop Marco

stealing the emeralds, Josh got into such a temper that he flung a vicious punch at the airman. Timmy knew Guy was his mistress's friend – so he went for the hijacker's throat! Josh let out a yell. George shouted at Timmy. The walls of the temple echoed with all the noise – and the Jivaros, thinking it was a call to them to come and help, rushed in!

Pſo was no fool. He might be superstitious, but he had a quick brain, and he didn't need any explanation of what was going on! The sight of the chisel in Marco's hands and several very obvious scratches round one of the golden idol's eyes was quite enough for him. He snapped out an order – and struggle as they might, the hijackers were soon overpowered. Two of the Jivaro porters came running in with creepers, and a moment later Josh, Marco and Luke were tied hand and foot.

Anne begged Pſo to untie Luke, but it was no good. He was angry enough with the hijackers for getting away from his village once already, so he was delighted to find them again. And he'd caught them red-handed trying to make off with the emeralds too! Attacking the moon goddess was a terrible crime in his eyes. The chief wouldn't even listen to his witch doctor – he decided that the three men who had tried to rob the temple must be taken back to the village and put to death at the time of the next new moon. However, Guy and the children were free to leave whenever they wanted. The chief had given his word, and he was going to keep it!

But the capture of Luke, Josh and Marco put Guy and the children in a terrible position. It was dreadful to think of leaving them to be sacrificed.

'I think all we can do just at the moment is go back to the village with the rest of the party,' said Guy. 'We'll need a few days' rest to get ready for our departure anyway. What's more, Pfo wants to have a great feast to celebrate the success of the expedition, and he's going to install the golden idol in my place in a big ceremony. Meanwhile I'll do my best to make the Jivaros change their minds, or find some way to get those three men out of their hands.'

Anne was crying quietly. She had become really fond of Luke, and she thought, quite rightly, that he was much less to blame than the other two for everything that had happened.

The whole party got back to the village quite easily, and the Jivaros carried the golden idol all the way, showing it the greatest respect. When they arrived in the clearing they shut the three prisoners up in the hut where they had been kept before, with a whole ring of men guarding them. Nobody kept watch on the Five any more, and at Guy's suggestion they moved into his big hut with him.

'But what can we do now, Guy?' George wondered out loud.

'Just what I've been asking myself!' said the airman ruefully. 'And however hard I rack my brains, I can't see *what* we're going to do to get your fine friends out of this mess!'

'But Luke really *is* a friend of mine!' Anne protested, not liking his sarcastic tone.

'Yes, yes, all right, Anne, but that isn't really the question. Now listen, children. First of all I want to get back to the crashed plane tonight and start broadcasting my SOS message again. After all, you never know your luck!'

And Guy was right to be hopeful. Back in the wrecked plane, he managed to get an answer to his distress signal at long last. His heart was thudding as he gave his distant contact a bearing on the position of the Jivaro village.

He woke the children up as soon as he got back. 'I did it!' he told them, delighted. 'Someone picked up my signal at last – I got in touch with some engineers working for a timber company, and they're going to alert the Brazilian authorities. I'll go back to the plane this evening, and I hope there'll be more good news then. I hardly dare to think of it, but the whole nightmare could be coming to an end!'

'My word – I hope help comes in time!' said Julian, sounding very worried. 'What I mean is, the new moon is only six days off!'

Guy hadn't forgotten that, but he still didn't see how they were going to save Luke and the other two from their dreadful fate. But in any case he had a good long rest that day, so as to be wide awake and alert when he went back to the plane in the evening.

'I shouldn't think an expedition could possibly get here within the next six days,' said Anne sadly, watching him leave the village again.

'If the worst does happen – for Luke and the others, I mean – we'll still be all right,' said Dick, trying to cheer her up. 'Guy can be our guide and help us out of the forest.'

But it was no use – poor Anne just burst into tears. She couldn't bear the thought of Luke dying.

Guy came back at dawn, in excellent spirits. 'It's all right!' he said. 'The news of our adventure has gone all over the world, and your parents know you're safe and sound!'

The children's eyes were shining as they waited to hear the rest of his news.

'Army helicopters will be on their way to find us within four days' time,' Guy went on. 'They'll pick us up and get us well away from here. We'll have to get a landing pad ready for them, of course. Even a helicopter can't come down in the middle of the jungle! But that shouldn't present any problems. I'll tell Pfo there are more messengers from heaven coming to pick us up, and he wouldn't dare go against the will of Kaloum-Kaloum!'

George and her cousins were delighted. They would soon be leaving! Their parents knew they were safe!

But then Anne asked, 'What about Luke and Josh and Marco?'

The smile faded from Guy's face. I'm sorry, Anne,' he said. 'I don't think there's anything we can do for them. The mere fact that you children are here will prevent the soldiers who are coming to fetch us from trying to rescue them by force, too. *You* might get hurt!'

'But surely the helicopters could come back after they've taken us to safety?' said Dick.

'I'm afraid the time's too tight for that – by the time they'd got here, and gone away, and come back again it would be too late. The sacrifice would have taken place. What's more, I don't think the Brazilian authorities really want to fight any of the Indian tribes, not without consulting all sorts of officials first. And you know how slowly that sort of thing goes – there wouldn't be any hope of action before the men were sacrificed.'

The Five weren't looking nearly so happy now. Even Timmy's ears were drooping and his tail was between his legs – the intelligent dog was very sensitive to the way the children felt! George clenched her fists.

'We *must* find a way to save them – we simply must!' she muttered.

She didn't sleep much that night – indeed, she didn't really drop off until morning, when she had an idea in her head. It was still a vague sort of idea, but she thought it was promising.

Next day she told Guy and her cousins, 'I've been thinking, and I believe I've found a way to get Luke and co. out of the awful mess they're in!'

'Well, come on, let's hear it!' said Julian. 'Don't keep us in suspense, George!'

'It's not all that simple,' said George. 'We'll need Guy's help – and Marco will have to learn his own part well!'

'Marco?' said Guy, sounding very surprised. 'What's *he* got to do with your plan?'

George explained. 'I remembered something from when we were all camping in the wreck of the plane. The evenings seemed very long, didn't they? Well, one day Luke asked Marco to amuse us with his ventriloquist act. And it turned out that Marco's quite a good ventriloquist – he can imitate voices and make it sound as if they come from all sorts of different places.'

'That's right!' Dick said. 'I remember now, too – he's very clever at it.'

'So I thought we could use Marco's talent for projecting his voice,' George went on. 'Suppose he could make the moon goddess herself talk . . . ?'

Guy sat up suddenly and looked hard at clever George. 'Why, that's a wonderful idea!' he said. 'Yes! Yes, I see just how to do it – now let's think! Yes, if I can persuade Pfo to confront the wrong-doers with the goddess they tried to insult, and I tell him she will decide their fate . . . then I can ask the idol questions, and Marco can answer them!'

Julian shook his head doubtfully. 'I'm afraid that won't work,' he said. 'The Jivaros don't know any language but their own, and Marco doesn't speak the Jivaro dialect.'

'Oh, we can get round that difficulty all right,' Guy told him. 'Jivaro is a concise sort of language, and the syllables that go to make it up are easy to pronounce. I'll get together with Marco, and he can learn the right replies for the goddess to make off by heart.'

Anne was delighted. 'Oh, Guy, oh, George, you're both wonderful!' she cried. 'Oh, I'm so happy! Our friends will be safe after all!'

Nobody bothered to point out that the hijackers weren't exactly 'friends' of theirs – there was too much else to do.

Guy wasted no time in going off to find Pfo, who thought it was quite natural for Kaloum-Kaloum, the god of the wind, to send machines with wings for Rna and the white children. As they'd all come from the sky they ought obviously to go back there. He ordered his Jivaro hunters to set to work at once clearing a landing pad to one side of the village.

Meanwhile the Jivaro women were putting up a sort of platform near the chief's hut. The idol with the emerald eyes was hoisted up on this platform, and Guy, in full witch doctor costume, held a great ceremony to welcome her to the village.

And now the villagers were only waiting for the new moon to sacrifice the three hijackers in the middle of the clearing. Guy had another earnest conversation with the chief.

'The goddess wishes to pass judgement on the men who profaned her temple herself,' he told Pfo.

Pfo accepted this without any difficulty – it seemed a perfectly natural thing for the goddess to want. So Guy wasted no time in going to see the prisoners. He found Josh and Marco very depressed indeed. Luke was more resigned to his fate, and was trying to cheer the others up, instead of moaning and groaning himself. All three were much surprised to see Rna the witch doctor followed by the Five.

'Come to gloat, have you?' said Josh in a nasty tone of voice.

'What an awful thing to say!' said Dick indignantly. 'We have *not* come to gloat – we've come to help you!'

Guy silenced him with a gesture, and then calmly told the three hijackers about the plan they had thought up to save them. . .

The morning of the ceremony came. George and her cousins watched it all, fascinated. The whole Jivaro tribe was gathered in the middle of the village. The golden idol shone in the first rays of the sun, the moon's husband. Rna stood beside the goddess. The children were the only ones who could guess how fast Guy's heart must be beating under his witch doctor's finery. Would he manage to save the hijackers?

Sitting on a special throne, Pfo watched the ceremony. He had his wife on one side of him and Tofi on the other. The Five were standing to one side. Timmy seemed to know what a serious moment this was, and he stood perfectly still beside his mistress. Suddenly Jivaro warriors led the three prisoners up. Josh didn't look good at all, but there was a certain dignity about Luke and even Marco.

Rna solemnly stepped forward to confront the three men. He pointed one arm threateningly in their direction and then turned to address the goddess at length. The Jivaros listened to what their witch doctor said in devout silence.

Once again the witch doctor pointed to the prisoners, and then stepped back, leaving them to face the idol.

Pfo craned his neck. The goddess herself was to pass judgement on the men who had tried to rob her temple. It was a solemn moment!

131

The witch doctor put his first question to the idol, in Jivaro, of course. 'O Goddess, do you know these men?' he cried.

George and her cousins could follow the sense of what he was saying, just as they could with all the other questions. And they knew the answers to his questions too – the ones Marco had to put into the idol's mouth.

'I only hope he doesn't mess it all up!' thought George. 'And most of all I hope the Jivaros don't suspect it's a trick!'

Suddenly the words she was waiting to hear emerged from the goddess's still lips. 'Yes, I know these men!'

A sort of thrill ran through the crowd. The Jivaros prostrated themselves. Unmoved, the witch doctor went on.

'Chief Pfo has condemned them to death. Do they deserve this punishment?'

'Yes,' replied the idol, 'they deserve it!'

'And how are they to die, O Goddess? Speak!'

Marco had to make quite a long speech now. If only he didn't start stammering or anything like that because of the tense situation! But it was all right! The goddess's golden lips pronounced sentence, speaking every word perfectly clearly.

'The evil-doers shall be sacrificed to the moon by Kaloum-Kaloum himself, in his kingdom of the winds! The condemned men must travel there with

Rna to face the wrath of Kaloum-Kaloum!'

Another thrill ran through the crowd as they took in the horror of this sentence. Pso slowly raised his hand.

'Very good!' he told the witch doctor. 'The goddess has spoken. Kaloum-Kaloum shall have his victims. Will you take them with you to his kingdom of the winds?'

'I will do as the goddess orders, Pso. You can rely on me!' said Guy, earnestly.

Entering into the spirit of the thing, Luke, Marco and Josh looked very downcast indeed. They were taken away. The children could hardly hide their joy, but they managed it somehow. In fact Anne was weeping quietly – only this time her tears were tears of relief! Julian was congratulating George on her clever trick, in an undertone.

Now all they had to do was wait for the Army helicopters to arrive! And on the day Guy had arranged, he and the children were anxiously watching the sky from the moment the sun rose. Suddenly they heard the familiar sound of an aircraft engine. One by one, the helicopters appeared above the forest, their rotors whirring in the air. The Jivaros had seen planes before, very high up above them, but never helicopters, so they didn't for a moment doubt that these amazing machines were ships sent down from the sky by Kaloum-Kaloum. They were all the more certain because the helicopters produced strong air currents when they touched down. It was just as if a violent wind were getting up – no doubt Kaloum-Kaloum himself was somewhere around, watching his messengers leave for his kingdom!

Guy quietly thanked heaven that Pfo's tribe was so cut off from the rest of the world, and clung so faithfully to its old superstitions. But for that, they would never have managed to escape the Jivaros!

The Indians all gathered to watch as a small procession made for the helicopters, walking quite slowly. The air crews on board had strict instructions: they weren't to land themselves, and they were not to let the Jivaros see them. Rna the witch doctor solemnly led Luke, Josh and Marco to the helicopters, pretending he had to force them to get in. The children turned to Pfo and Tofi, who were standing at a respectful distance to watch them leave. They waved goodbye before they too climbed into the helicopters.

George and Dick got into the same one. 'Woof!' said Timmy, climbing in after his young mistress.

Rna the witch doctor was the last to get ready to go up to the sky again. Solemn and straight-faced as ever, he signed to Pfo to come closer, and when the chief was beside him, Guy took off his mask.

'You must keep this, Pfo, in memory of my departure,' he said. 'Take good care of the moon goddess. She will protect you and yours – and now goodbye!'

For the first time that day, Pſo showed a trace of emotion. He was really fond of his witch doctor. Rna climbed into the helicopter, and the machines took off, one after the other. The Jivaros craned their necks to watch them fly away. Nose pressed to the glass of the porthole, George looked down at the village below her. She could see the golden idol on the platform, the Jivaros gathered round the landing pad, the indistinct figures of Pſo and Tofi.

The helicopter turned towards the forest and the Jivaro village disappeared from sight. George sighed.

'Well, that's it,' she told Dick. 'The adventure's over – but it *was* an adventure, wasn't it?'

'You can say that again!' Dick assured her.

They had a smooth journey, and reached an Army airfield just as planned. The passengers got into different helicopters, and at their next stop they found a plane waiting for them. The whole party boarded this plane – and flew on to Manao, and from Manao straight to Rio.

It was the first time all of them had been together since they took off from the Jivaro village. Josh was withdrawn and silent. He knew the police would be waiting for him and his friends in Rio. Luke and Marco, however, thanked Guy and the children warmly for saving their lives.

And at last, next day, they actually arrived in

Rio. There was a wonderful surprise for the Five! Aunt Fanny and Uncle Quentin, and Julian, Dick and Anne's own parents, had all come to Brazil to meet them – they just couldn't wait for them to get back to England before they were all reunited.

It was a wonderful moment for all of them! And there was a pleasant surprise for Guy, too. His return from the dead had made exciting news in the world of aviation, and lots of his former colleagues were waiting to welcome him back.

He and the Five had to pose for photograph after photograph. George smiled when she saw that Timmy seemed to be posing for the photographers too, on purpose! He'd be in all the papers tomorrow as well.

The children's parents decided that they would all spend a couple of weeks in Brazil – after all, the Five still hadn't had the holiday they'd been promised. And then they would fly back to England together.

Three days after they got back to Kirrin, George and her cousins had news of Guy, who was back in England himself by now. He sent them his love, and promised to come and see them soon.

As for the trial of the hijackers, it took place a bit later, at the beginning of next school term. George, Julian, Dick and Anne all had to go and give evidence, and so did Guy, so they all met again then. Thanks to the children's evidence, Luke only got a light jail sentence, and he assured the judge that once he'd served it he would go straight and, earn an honest living. As for Josh and Marco, they were sent to prison for quite a long time, as they deserved.

There was a touching scene after the trial, when Luke was allowed to see the children and Guy and thank them for their evidence in his favour.

'And now,' said George happily, as they left the court, 'now for the *next* adventure! I do wonder what it will be?'

If you have enjoyed this book you may like to read some more exciting adventures from Knight Books. Here is a complete list of Enid Blyton's FAMOUS FIVE adventures:

WILLARD PRICE

A complete list of his thrilling animal adventures:

Hal and Roger Hunt are sent all over the world by their father in search of rare animals with which to supply zoos. Their adventures on the way are full of action and suspense and every book is packed with information about the remoter regions of the earth, together with encyclopaedic facts about the world's animal kingdom.

KNIGHT BOOKS

NICHOLAS FISK

THE STARSTORMER SAGA

Starstormers
Sunburst
Catfang
Evil Eye
Volcano

The four Starstormers are Vawn, Ispex, Tsu and
Makenzi. They construct a spaceship from pieces
of scrap and, together with their robot Shambles,
take off into deepest space. *Starstormer* takes them
into a thrilling series of space adventures, including strange encounters on alien planets and a con-
tinual and dangerous battle against the wicked
Octopus Emperor.

KNIGHT BOOKS